VENTURE BEYOND

Stories from Hidden Worlds- Collection 1

K.R. Stevens

ISBN-13: 9798272059529

Cover design by: K.R. Stevens
Art by: Inessa Burnell
Library of Congress Control Number: 2018675309
Printed in the United States of America

CONTENTS

Title Page

Copyright

Introduction

The Bones of Night   1

The Bones of Night #1   2

The Bones of Night #2   6

The Bones of Night #3   11

Avalon Academy   18

Avalon Academy #1   19

Avalon Academy #2   28

Avalon Academy #3   33

Defiant Horizon   43

Prologue   44

Defiant Horizon #1   55

Defiant Horizon #2   68

Defiant Horizon #3   83

INTRODUCTION

Take a chance on Stories from Hidden Worlds - Collection 1. Enjoy three issues each from three of my short story series, and find your new favorite series to follow! Journey to fabled lands, nightmare realms, and visions of a future from a world not unlike our own. There is so much discover, you just need to take that first step.

-Avalon Academy of the Arcane-

Journey to the fabled shores of Avalon Academy in a fantasy slice-of-life story that follows various students and staff at a magic school held just out of sight from the rest of the world. Explore enchanting ancient ruins, fearsome powers, but, most importantly, the interconnected lives of the people who live there.

Meet students like Abigail, a stranger to Avalon who discovered the Academy by accident, though things rarely happen by accident in Avalon. Or, follow staff like Headmistress Lauren Corvinus, who is investigating a mystery that could unlock some of the deepest secrets of Avalon.

-The Bones of Night-

Dive into the bleak future of The Bones of Night, a dark sci-fi, cassette futurist horror series that asks you to discover what caused the disappearance of the crew of a space mining ship, through only the logs of the crew. Can you trust the company that owns the ship to be sending you everything? Can you even trust that the crew is telling the truth? After all, the logs only get more bizarre the more you listen.

Can you solve the mystery of the *Prospector*?

-Defiant Horizon-

In a cyberpunk superhero story 20 years in the making, rise up in Defiant Horizon. Step into the hologram-soaked streets of Hashishima, the financial and technological capital of the world, as the various global superpowers vie for control. As war seems inevitable, people with superhuman abilities begin to rise. Will they be able to save the independent island nation of Hashishima from being swallowed in the fires of global conflict? Or will they pursue their own selfish, and even dark ends.

Follow characters like Monica, a Lieutenant in the Hashishima Police Force who is searching for superhumans, and trying to bring those who commit crimes to justice. Or Amanda, the head of Marshall-Saito Technologies, who is determined to find the mythical Kuroi Kitsune, the fabled avenging spirit of Hashishima who may be more fact than fiction. Or Marko, the creator of Byakko Industries, who is hell-bent on revenge after an unknown rival sends mercenaries to attack his company.

THE BONES OF NIGHT

The Bones of Night is a Dark Sci-Fi Horror short story series where you must uncover what happened to the crew of a space mining ship, through only the logs of the crew. Can you solve the mystery of The Prospector?

THE BONES OF NIGHT #1

The Return

Hello Investigator,

Per your request, and in cooperation with the Office of Loss Prevention and Incident Management, I have attached here a packet of data from the log files from the Prospector, formerly known as the Pickaxe.

As we discussed before, the main computer core suffered from significant data corruption the likes of which we haven't seen before. Our engineers are still working on recovering any data we can to understand what happened. Unfortunately this is all Frontier Dynamics has been able to piece together so far.

It looks unlikely that we will be able to recover video surveillance, or much of the sensor data as these are the most heavily corrupted partitions. We will, of course, make every effort to get whatever we can. The crew personal logs appear to be the least damaged, so we hope that they may help to elucidate what happened on the ship in lieu of the more ideal data that is very likely permanently lost.

We will continue to send any data recovered as we get it.

Respectfully,

Margaret Aurelius
Director of Deep Space Mining Initiatives and Exploration
Frontier Dynamics Corporation, Interstellar

Mission Day -8

Executive Officer Kazuhiro Inaba

Now that we are in Quicknet range of Exchange Station 7, Cap's been talking with Frontier Dynamics about our next gig. Sounds like they are extending the contract by another three, maybe even six months, which is great. By law we get to renegotiate shares for the crew, which we could really use a bump after Cap lowballed us to get this job in the first place. Plus, since it's a contract extension, we don't need to pack up any time soon. They'll just keep us on the same boat.

That's fine by me, I just got used to my bunk, even with the weird dip in the middle. The hum of the ship's systems feel like home now. I always hate having to go to a new ship at the end of a contract. I mean, it's part of the job, the boats belong to the company, we are just the rats catching a ride and doing the work. It's just that it'd be really nice to be nailed to a ship for more than a couple hauls.

Who knows, if this new dig Cap's been trying to get us on works out, we could be cozy on the Pick for awhile.

Mission Day -7

Engineering Chief David Madsen

XO Kaz just told me Cap's got us signed up for another dig already. I told him we need to bring the Pick in for a reactor overhaul at the end of the haul. The stardrive primary heatsink might as well be slag with how stressed it is. If it fails, we still have the secondary and tertiary heatsinks, but that'll kick down drive efficiency 50%, turning a three month trip into a three year one, if not more. Hell, half the secondary systems are being held together with duct tape and spite. That, by the way, includes life support. Who cares if the crew dies from choking on their own carbon dioxide as long as the computer can bring the ship back on it's own, right?

The Pick is in serious need of maintenance. Another haul could be a danger to the whole crew, even the ship itself. Cap knows it, yet he's still lining up another dig? If he won't do what needs to be done, I will.

One report to the Maintenance and Flight Safety Bureau will ground the Pickaxe till she can get buttoned up. I don't need to die over this shit.

Mission Day -7

Security Personnel Meredith Andrews

Well it's official, Cap announced we have another haul after this one. Happy that I don't have to bid for a new post when we get in, can't say I'm enthused about another tour with this lot of rockmunchers and pricks, but at least after what happened with Simmons they know not to fuck with the pretty blonde with a mean right hook and a gun.

What worries me is these losers have been on back-to-back jobs for like a year and a half. Most of them have been itching for a chance to blow some scrip, blow some loads, and blow off some steam. Another 6-7 months isn't going to make my job easy. Maybe we need to req some extra booze, or Clarity to take some of the edge off. Yeah, there'll probably be more fights, but might keep them from killing each other, or worse.

Who knows, maybe I'll have to prove once again that the mess hall is rigged with tear gas and sonic suppression turrets. They didn't step out of line for weeks last time.

Mission Day -7

Sanitation Technician Chip Ross

Jesus, do I wish Fisk would stop clogging the heads. Don't know what crawled inside that boy an' died, but whatever did musta turned his guts into a super glue factory. I have never seen someone who could clog a toilet almost every time he uses it.

Damn, boy.

I've got the waste system set to Collection so we can sell everybody's shit. Still find it funny just how much of our paycheck at the end of a job comes from our sewage and trash. I heard from an accountant once that the recycle credits FD gets from the Collective makes them more than the whole crew gets paid and then some for a job.

Worth less than junk, not that that's a surprise. When you work with rigs that process and repurpose people's shit every day for long enough, you stop thinking you are much better than it.

THE BONES OF NIGHT #2

The Report

Hello, Investigator,

Enclosed is a new packet of data our engineers have been able to recover from the corrupted computer core.

I know you are likely hoping for more recent logs that should provide more insight into what the incident was aboard the Prospector, formerly known as the Pickaxe. However, the data corruption seems to progressively worsen the younger the files are. It will take a significant amount of time to reconstruct these files, if they can be at all.

I wanted to let you know that the Inspection Team's initial report should be completed by my next message with details on their preliminary findings before they go through the ship with advanced scanning equipment. Hopefully this will assist in shedding more light on what happened.

I appreciate your patience in the meantime. I will send more when I am able.

Respectfully,

Margaret Aurelius
Director of Deep Space Mining Initiatives and Exploration
Frontier Dynamics Corporation, Interstellar

Mission Day -7

Excavation Operator Nathan Fisk

Well, shit. Here I was hoping I'd have a chance to get some action when we pull into station. Nah, Cap's gone and signed us up for a new gig. Fuck.

Jesus Christ, what I wouldn't give for a night at Sandy's Dollhouse.

Still, more work is more work. Gotta pay off my loan from the Syndicate somehow, mother fuckers.

Mission Day -7

Flight Officer Dean Castillo

Cap's got us on the hook for a brand new system, LQI-8779, that hasn't been touched yet. Looks like the only data we have on it is from an old probe from the Wesley Expeditions Theta Sector Mapping missions back, geez, almost 100 years ago.

Typical binary red dwarf system, nothing special there. Four planets. Alpha is a massive hot Jupiter type, but no moons. No money there, but maybe a Gas Rig could get some scratch there. Beta 1 and 2 look like dirt balls that may have been the same planet at some point, but now are two tidally locked rocks with a decaying orbit. We'll have to take some intensive scans of these two during the dig since the probe seemed to only get a limited amount of data on them. Could be a gold mine. Gamma is probably the largest ice giant I've ever seen and has more satellites than the probe could count in it's brief flyby. Will probably get a nice bonus if I can map the whole system while we are deployed.

We're being sent to the largest satellite the probe observed around Gamma. It's a large rocky moon with a huge amount of heavy metals. They are calling it Site A, since the probe didn't map enough of Gamma's satellites to be able to give it an official GSPSS designation. The probe got a pretty decent scan of the surface with some very promising results.

Personally, I'm just happy we are going somewhere no one's ever been to before. I'm gonna to make a fortune on charts and survey scans alone, even if I have to go to the 'secondary' market.

Mission Day -6

Captain Hans Singh

Well, Madsen's really done it now. He actually sent a report to Collective Maintenance and Flight Safety Bureau flagging the Pick as a "Danger to Crew and Vessel Alike". FD is furious. They are threatening not only to cancel the contract, but flag every crew member as non-rehireable. What the fuck was he thinking?

The moment we dock at Exchange Station 7, Collective agents will flood the boat for an inspection and we'll be grounded till every fault is fixed. This will cost Frontier Dynamics trillions of unicreds. Hell, another Exo-Mining Corp could takeover the claim on the system we were supposed to be digging.

This is so fucked up. 20 years, a nearly flawless record, and next in line for promotion to Regional Operations Manager, and it's all about to come crashing down because a glorified grease monkey can't keep his damn mouth shut. Even if he rescinds his report, we'll be inspected anyway just because the ship was flagged to begin with.

What the fuck am I going to do.

Mission Day -6

Security Personnel Meredith Andrews

For fuck's sake. I know Cap was furious about what Madsen did to fuck over the next gig, but he didn't need to sock him so hard he dislocated Chief's jaw. What the hell am I supposed to do, lock the Captain in the brig? A full brawl almost broke out in the mess hall till I threatened to pull the tear gas on them.

I've got them both confined to quarters till FD can tell me what the protocol for this kind of situation is. Usually, on deployment, out of People's Star Collective's formally recognized territory, ships function under Frontier Law. The ship's captain *is* the law. But we are close enough to Collective space that Frontier Law may not apply. So, all I can do right now is wait for their FD's lawyers to get back with my next step.

In the meantime, XO Kaz is in charge. The crew likes him, at least, so hopefully that's the most eventful the next 5 days are before we make Exchange Station 7.

Mission Day -6

Medical Operator Dr. Frederick Saginaw, MD

New patient, Madsen. Dislocated jaw, 2 cracked ribs. Got him set. Got him some meds, and have him sleeping it off for now. Will give him a check in the morning before release back to work.

Mission Day -6

Quartermaster Harlan Green

Alrighty, I have officially lifted rationing of booze and mood enhancers since we are in the home stretch. I guess I had miscalculated consumption rates when I set ration limits for the mission, and we somehow have a 10-day surplus. Might as well let everyone live a little before we get back on station.

I'm getting a want/need list for resupply for the next gig together since Cap just announced it. I sent a heads up to the department leads to get what they want.n I know Chip was saying before he needed more air filters this time, since we were really stretching this time. Also Dr. Mulgrew already put in a request for more sonic drill bits, det charges, and bunch of other mining kit. Glad to see him thinking ahead for a change. Usually, I have to beg him to send me his requisition list up till the last second. Maybe he finally got tired of me nagging him.

THE BONES OF NIGHT #3

The Prospector

Hello, Investigator,

Here is the next data packet our engineers have been able to recover. I also have the preliminary inspection report I mentioned last time from our inspection team attached.

I would like to preface this set of logs by admitting that there is some, well, sensitive information enclosed that would not be received well if released to the public. I would advise an appropriate level of restraint and discretion with this, in accordance with our arrangement with your Director Fitzgerald.

Should you have any questions, or doubts as to our willingness to... cooperate with the smooth procedure of this investigation, please feel free to contact my office on a Level 6 encrypted line, or higher. It would be my pleasure to put those doubts to rest.

Respectfully,

Margaret Aurelius
Director of Deep Space Mining Initiatives and Exploration
Frontier Dynamics Corporation, Interstellar

Preliminary Briefing on Official Loss

Investigation Inspection Report for
The Prospector,
CCV-07210110810809811111171101
00

Loss Incident – 5761746368696E67a

Reporting Inspection Officer Bryce Tamlin

This report is a record of findings from the initial sweep through *The Prospector.* Bear in mind that this is an ongoing inspection, and details may change over time as more evidence comes to light. Hopefully this report will give some clues so as to answer the cause of the loss of crew incident on *The Prospector*.

This is a Frontier Dynamics DSE-427 Delver Class Deep Space Mining Vessel originally commissioned in 2194. According to Frontier Dynamics records, it has run 2,020 missions. True flight time in unclear at this time as the team working on data recovery has yet to piece the flight computer together. But upon the last logged true flight time from the last time the ship docked, it has put in about 326 years of service between time experienced in the Threshold, and out. It should be noted that Delver classes are rated for 200 years of service before a major refit and overhaul is required, or the ship designated for salvage. We have yet to see any record of either of these being scheduled for the ship, so it is possible that insufficient maintenance could have been a contributing factor to the loss incident.

Recovery Location

The Prospector was found adrift about .5 lightyears outside of the Korazki Ditch. The main computer initiated an automatic distress beacon when it couldn't activate its sublight drive. Strangely enough, the recovery team was able to initiate the drive for a deceleration burn once they boarded the ship. It is possible that the computer core corruption had disabled the automatic flight systems, but that is still unclear at this time.

Recovery Conditions

It appears the main computer sustained significant data corruption. As previously mentioned, we are unable access the flight data, or the computer's internal chronometer. We hope to have more information for the full inspection briefing later.

What we can tell is that the ship did a Threshold dive back, whether directed to, or driven automatically by the computer. We cannot ascertain the conditions the ship entered the Threshold in, but we can tell that the primary and secondary heat sinks suffered catastrophic damage, kicking down drive efficiency to approximately 17%. The fact that the main reactor didn't detonate due to overheating is no small miracle.

However long the ship was in the Threshold for, it had to have been a very long time. All functions non-essential to drive operations had been shut down. The vessel seemed to be operating for so long that nearly all of the reactor fuel has been consumed. By rough estimates from the remaining viable fuel rods, if the ship had spent a couple more years in the Threshold, it is very possible that the reactor would have deactivated, the shield would have dropped, and the vessel would have been consumed by the Infradimensonal Plane.

It should be noted that the damage to the main computer core is absolutely unprecedented. The Data Recovery team says they have never seen anything like it.

General Condition

The ship is intact, save for the loss of the heat sinks. There is significant scoring on the hull in certain pockets consistent with passing through a micrometeorite cloud without shields, but no breaches. It looks like the primary heat sink had been rigged to dissipate excess heat through the shield matrix, as well as what we assume were connections to the heat sinks for the lander and the emergency shuttle, but with both of those missing, we can't say so conclusively.

The metal interior feels almost plastic-like. Not like the tough steel composite you might expect. Overall, the ship feels, frankly, ancient. Dust covers every flat surface. The rubber components are all brittle, and shatter to dust on contact. Even the bulkheads and wall partitions seem to be bowed, and freckled with corrosion. Conditions like this are roughly consistent with derelicts that have been abandoned for over a hundred years or so, but we have seen instances where anomalies at high aspect FTL have caused similar structural decay in localized areas.

Crew Conditions

We were unable to locate any of the crew, nor any identifiable remains so far. Using the personnel locators is currently impossible with the state the computer is in. So, that means we get to do things the hard way. We have checked through much of the Command and Crew module of the ship, but there's a significant area in the Engineering and Cargo modules, including those without atmosphere, that we have yet to be able to check. By the next briefing, we will have a full multi-spectral scan of the ship to get a better idea of what happened.

We have sent Sparrow drones to see if, perhaps, the crew were all down on the surface, and had to, for some unclear reason, abandon ship. But the drones have yet to return, even though they are a month past their return window.

Assumed total loss of crew, but the inspection is still ongoing. We will be in touch as soon as we can with a more thorough briefing.

Mission Day -4

Captain Hans Singh

Word came in from the Frontier Dynamics legal team. They say they're considering the spat I had with Madsen under Frontier Law, as long as he doesn't try to press charges. Looks like he's declined to. So, back to business as usual.

Talked with Margaret, and it looks like we might have a solution to our other problem the Chief caused. FD is changing the ship registry for the Pick. Tomorrow, when we pull into Exchange Station 7, we will be docking as the Prospector, CCV-0721011081080981111117110100. I've got Kaz tweaking the transponder now. No issues with Flight and Safety, no Collective agents, all clear. Can't imagine who or how much FD had to pay to get to look the other way, but I'm sure some high level administrator just got enough scrip to retire early.

Chief Madsen has been bumped down half of his share for the haul we are bringing in. That's a lot of money, but a pretty light punishment for what he pulled. They are probably just hoping he doesn't try anything else in the meantime

Well, it's time to get on the ship wide and announce the new job is back on! That'll certainly get morale back up.

Mission Day -4

Engineering Technician Walter Travis

Oh, this doesn't feel right. My family's been working on boats for generations. Brine and seafoam is practically part of my blood. If there's one thing you learn from a family with a history like mine, you never change the name of your ship. It's bad luck. Great Grandfather Leland's ship sunk the day after he renamed it to the

Scallywag. Sure, this is a space ship, but a boat is a boat. It just doesn't sit right with me.

Worst of all, Madsen made me EVA and repaint the name and registry number to match the transponder. I feel like I've been doubly cursed. Not only on a cursed ship, but I'm now the one that done it.

No good will come of this. I'm going to pray.

Mission Day -4

Security Personnel Meredith Andrews

You can practically feel the whole ship sigh with relief. Dear God, I thought the crew was about to eat each other after how tense the last couple of days have been.

Seems like the whole situation with Cap and the Chief was enough to distract everyone from the fact that we aren't getting a break on station. Sounds like once we unload and restock, FD wants us en route to the next dig.

Whatever. As long as these idiots aren't causing trouble, I don't give a shit. I need the money. Thought for sure this incident with Madsen would put me behind on my payments.

Don't want to imagine what the Syndicate would do with me if I did. Probably no where near as bad as what the government would do if the Syndicate hadn't paid my tax and loss recovery fines from those two digs that went bust. But, hell, that's ancient history by now.

Mission Day -3

Quartermaster Harlan Green

I swear, FD is trying to bankrupt us with what they charge for supplies. The price of basic rations has shot up 35% since we last resupplied. It's a fact, I checked the PO. And that's just basic rations, you know, what we eat in a emergency. Basically just protein paste and algae hardtack. Real food is even worse.

Thankfully the renegotiated contract that Cap worked out upped our requisition allowances. But I think we'll have less food, air, and water than we did last time. We can use recyclers to stretch that out, but the crew isn't going to like it. No one wants to eat something they just shit out last night. Especially with that awful cough syrup taste the recyclers, for some ungodly reason, mix in.

Well, I could always talk with my friend who is part of the local Syndicate. Maybe I can get some supplies for a better price under the table. FD doesn't care how you spend requisition scrip as long as your crew is alive. Hell, the Syndicate probably pays them to look the other way anyway. Who knows, maybe we can get some burgers made with real beef, instead of that synthesized crap. That would sure keep the crew happy, and off my back.

AVALON ACADEMY

Avalon Academy of the Arcane is a Magical Slice-of-Life short story series that follows the daily lives of various students and staff at a magic school housed on the wandering island of Avalon.

AVALON ACADEMY #1

Outsider

Abigail

Abby peeked around the corner of the old Greyson Mill building just outside of the city. Two figures, a young man and a young woman stood in front of a doorway that stood alone from the rubble that surrounded it. They were chatting excitedly, though she couldn't quite hear what they were saying.

The two were strangely dressed, especially for this end of town. The girl had dark hair, and wore a blue silk... robe, or coat, with intricate embroidery, over a fine white blouse, brown vest, and skirt. When the girl had passed Abby before, she could make out some strange, unrecognizable markings along the hemline. The boy, who seemed a bit younger, wore what looked to be a kind of formal grey military coat with a purple silk sash and cape.

Take away the coat or cape, and perhaps they might look somewhat normal, if a bit finely dressed for such a dilapidated area. But... she'd never seen anyone dressed like they were. Abby just had to know what they were up to.

Perhaps the most puzzling thing was that no one else seemed to share her curiosity. Even Carl the Knife left them alone as they walked right in front of him over at the old bank building. Fine clothes like that were just asking to be robbed by any number of desperate dregs in this town. Yet, these two strolled by without a care in the world for the past week, and no one but her even lifted an eyebrow.

The girl took out a long, thin, metal rod from her purse, showing it off to the boy, who marveled at it. The girl smirked and shrugged, obviously trying to play as if it were nothing so grand, but Abby could see from even as far away as she was that how the girl smiled, and held the rod, told how she really felt. This was something precious. The boy's reaction was more than enough to confirm that.

Suddenly, they drew out their pocket watches, gold casings glinting in the slowly growing sunlight from above, and the two locked eyes. The boy reached into his pockets and pulled out something. Then he turned to the door, opened it, and the two walked through. The door closed briskly behind them.

Abby cautiously stepped over to the door from her hiding place. Like some kind of forlorn monument to the what she heard used to be the office building that used to stand there, the door stood alone. She looked behind the door and saw only rubble, dust, and the occasional patch of moss. The pair were nowhere to be seen. She grinned. They had been going *somewhere*, just like she had thought. The real question was *where*.

She placed her hand on the old door knob and tried to turn it. However, the knob was stuck fast and wouldn't budge. Abby looked over the door closely. There was a keyhole in the knob. Perhaps that was what the young man had taken out of his pocket, a key. She crouched down so that the door knob was level with her eyes and considered it for a moment. Something told her that even if she could pick the lock, it wouldn't make a difference. Forcing the lock open seemed a bad choice as well. The door frame looked to stand precariously as it was, robbed of a wall to hold it.

Abigail sighed, standing back up straight. She had seen the pair coming here for the past week, talking about wild, magnificent things. She thought it strange that she couldn't find them again until they left at night. Now she understood why. It should feel bizarre to find out that they were stepping through a door to, well, she couldn't say where. Wherever it went, it wasn't where it should be going, the other side of a ruined building. Wherever it went, it was anywhere but here.

Perhaps she could sneak in when they came tomorrow. She wasn't sure how, short of some sort of confrontation. Something inside her told her to try the door again. It was a silly thought. The doorknob wouldn't budge at all. Still, she decided to indulge the thought.

Her thin fingers wrapped around the cold, corroded brass knob, and she tried to turn it. But, unlike before, the knob twisted, slid the bolt out of the frame, and the door swung open. A cool, earthy breeze breathed out as the door opened.

Through the threshold, she could see a smooth stone corridor with a bright light at the end. With the door still open, she looked around the door from the outside again. There was nothing behind the door but open air and a pile of rubble. She came back to the opening, checking to make sure she hadn't imagined what she saw before. Yet, there was the stone corridor that shouldn't exist. It was impossible, nonsensical, and surely meant she was just seeing things. Somehow it felt... right, familiar even.

Abby grinned, and eagerly stepped through the threshold.

It took a moment for her eyes to adjust to the relative gloom of the corridor. She looked back just in time to see the door slam itself shut, and then fade into the stone wall that held it on this side. She couldn't help but chuckle. It would seem she was well past the point of no return.

Carefully, she walked towards the bright light at the end of the corridor. A cool breeze kissed her cheeks as she came closer. Then, she could finally see a field of green through the glare of the light beyond.

Abigail took her first step into the new land and was overcome with wonder at the sight before her. She stood in a vast rolling grassland dotted with what looked to be old stone buildings or ruins littered about the territory. A thick forest bordered to her left, and a single impressively tall mountain stood to her right. She thought she could see a lake, or some other body of water just at the edge of what she could make out across the grassland. She turned around and was confronted with an imposing cliff face. Various cutouts and reliefs could be seen in the grey stone. Hers was not the only tunnel, it seemed, that dug into the cliff. There were perhaps a dozen stone archways that were carved from the rippling stone to her left and right.

As she marveled at the sight, Abby heard the sound of a throat clearing behind her. She whipped around to see the slender figure of a beautiful middle-aged woman with long, curly, orangey-red hair that undulated in the breeze. The woman frowned, looking at a stone tablet in her hand, and spoke in a husky British accent. "Not in uniform, unbathed, and late to boot, I see. Your name, child?"

Abby blushed profusely, and took a step back towards the stone corridor. "I, uh…"

The woman raised an eyebrow, the look all the more menacing on her sharp, aquiline features. "I Uh. My, what *intriguing* names parents think of these days."

"It's not, um," Abigail stammered. "Ill just be leaving!" At that, she broke into a sprint down the corridor. When she reached the stone wall, she cursed to herself, having forgotten that the door had disappeared behind her. She hastily looked and probed about the wall, trying to find some hint of the door, or way to get back.

"Why not use your key, child, if you are so intent on escape?" Came the woman's voice from behind her again.

Defeated, Abigail turned around, and lowered her head. "I… don't have one."

She could see the woman's posture shift, putting more weight on her right side. "Really? Forgot that as well, did you? Leaving artifacts like that unattended can be quite dangerous, you know?"

"No, Ma'am... I – I don't have one at all." She looked back up to meet the woman's eyes, embarrassment flushing hot over her face till she felt close to bursting into flames.

"But how co..." the woman started, then her sharp green eyes narrowed. She lowered the tablet. "An outsider... But how... how did you get here?"

"I followed a boy and a girl talking about amazing things who I noticed coming to the same place around this time every day, and watched to see where they went. I was curious, you see? I – I saw them go through the door of a ruined office building next to the old Greyson mill, and just disappear." Abigail looked down at her feet. "Once they left, I tried to open the door and it... it just opened."

"Impossible..." the older woman said. She shifted her weight again to the other side. "Your name, young lady?"

Abby looked back up to meet the woman's piercing gaze. "Abigail Scot. I'm sorry for intruding. Truly. I'll j—." The woman raised her hand and shook her head. Her instincts, and something in the woman's eyes told Abby it was unwise to say anything further. She never ignored her instincts.

She grabbed Abby's hand, and marched out of the corridor. It was difficult for her to keep up with the older woman's longer legs, and purposeful stride. But, she managed to without tripping or lagging too far behind. Just what had she gotten herself into? It was far from the first time she had slipped in somewhere she didn't belong. Strangely enough, something told her she was exactly where she should be. She felt an uncanny sense that she had been in this place before. A sense that, somehow, this was her home. The very notion of feeling at home anywhere was foreign to her, but she couldn't shake impression.

They strode through the grassy hills, around the forest's edge, till they came to the marvelous sight of a network of buildings huddled to the side of a crystal clear lake. There were a dozen or so structures, a tall, crisp modern brick tower stood near the middle and was the tallest of them, but she could see buildings of various styles and apparent age mixed together. Some resembled drawings she had seen of old Roman or Greek temples. Others were more Gothic, like old cathedrals. She had never seen anything like the collection, even in her dreams.

The two pressed on, the older woman never breaking her brisk, unrelenting pace, till they entered what looked to be the oldest structure she had seen so far. Well, less a structure than what seemed to be a cave carved into a large rocky outcrop that framed the cluster of buildings opposite of the lake. Strange incense mixed with an ever-present sting of earth filled her nose. Unfamiliar markings and paintings lined the hewn stone walls, spun into a blur by how fast the woman pulled her along.

Abigail's legs were on fire, nearly on the verge of giving out by the time they blessedly came to a stop in a wide open chamber. Motes of light drifted between stalactites, illuminating what had to be a natural cavern. A still pool of water, like a sheet of glass sat at the far side of the chamber.

The woman looked back to her, those piercing eyes digging into her again. But, there was something different in them this time that Abby couldn't read. That terrified her. She prided herself on being able to understand what people were thinking. It had been a kind of gift of hers that had kept her safe all those years since...

A man with thick spectacles, and the thickest salt and pepper beard Abby had ever seen walked up from behind the woman. He was somewhat shorter than the woman was, but still taller than Abby by a head and a half. He had an accent that sounded somewhat vaguely European, but she couldn't put her finger on where. "Now, Lauren, who do you have in your talons today? Not often that we bring students in for being out of uniform."

"She is not a student, Ferrus." The woman said, looking to the man.

He adjusted his spectacles, and looked at Abby again. "Are you quite sure? She looks like one to me. Her aura is fierce, unbridled.

Like so many her age."

"Quite. I thought the same. But she isn't a student. She followed some students in."

"How could she do that without a key?" the man said. His dark cloud of a beard completely obscured his mouth, making it seem as though the wiggling of the beard itself was what produced his words.

"Exactly my question, Ferrus." The woman, whom the man had called Lauren, said.

Another voice came from behind in an unidentifiable accent, "unless she was let in by the three?" Abigail whipped her head around to see a clean-shaven man with coppery skin that had a metallic sheen to it.

"Nonsense, Something like that hasn't happened in centuries. There's no need. They've directed us to enroll likely prospects since, what. The first crusade?" Ferrus remarked.

Lauren didn't seem to share the same thought, but said nothing. That unreadable look was in her eyes as she looked back to Abby. Then she smiled? After seeing nothing but what seemed to be the woman's naturally stern, almost predatory visage, the sight of a smile curl on her aquiline features seemed almost incongruous.

The man stepped closer. He was a mountain of a man, impressively tall, easily the tallest of the group, and probably double Abby's height. Even through his simple suit, she could see that he might have been the most well-muscled men she had ever seen. "Your name, young lady?"

"It is Abigail Scot," she said, shifting uneasily. She never liked being the center of attention. The strangeness of the situation, and really everything since she had decided to follow the two, apparently, students, did not help set her at ease.

He smirked. "Could you tell me of your family, Ms. Scot?"

"I'm alone. My...they." Abby shook her head. "I'm sorry. I don't...

don't remember much about them."

Lauren and the strange man shared a look as Abby lowered her eyes in embarrassment.

The older woman spoke again, "I'd like you to try something for me. Let's call it a test."

Abigail's eyes shot back up as Lauren held out a small glass sphere. "What do…"

"Take this in both hands, close your eyes, and try to clear your mind," The older woman said softly.

She did as instructed, the last step, of course, much more difficult than it sounded. She had never been particularly great at "clearing her mind" of anything, especially not in this moment.

"Now, I want you to open your eyes, and focus on the sphere in your hands. I want you to think about the *most* important thing in the world to you, the thing that gets you out of bed every morning, or keeps you striving even when you want to give up." Lauren cleared her throat, and then continued. "Dig deep, really find that spark. It usually boils down to a single word, idea, or phrase. Once you find that thing, I want you to put it into that sphere"

"Put it in how?" Abby asked, raising an eyebrow.

Lauren smiled warmly in a way that seemed to instantly ease her anxiety. "You will know how, or you won't. It is as simple as that."

"How will I know if it worked?"

"Oh, that." Lauren grinned. "Believe me, there will be no doubt."

Abby looked back at the sphere, confused, but intrigued. What was the most important thing to her? Survival? Wouldn't that be the most important thing for anyone? No, people did things every day that was contrary to their survival, she had seen it herself sleeping on the streets of Old Town. No, Survival was just an easy answer. If Survival was the most important thing to her, why would she waste her time following those students when she could have been trying to give enough money to eat?

What was the most important thing to her? Why would she do something that would run against her survival? What did she want from that? What did she hope for in stepping through that door?

Change. The word ripped through her like a gust of wind blasting away stale air. That was what she desired more than anything else, to change. To get away from the life she had been living. To be something more.

Suddenly she could feel the thought coursing through her veins, pushing her forward. But forward to where? Her eyes locked onto the sphere, and in that moment she understood. Abigail pushed the idea into the sphere with her raw desire and hopes, and before her eyes, the sphere sparked into life. A roiling, surging cloud filled the inside of the sphere, twisting and contorting into a cyclone that somehow, she knew, represented Change.

She looked up to the older woman, and Lauren smiled. "Congratulations, my newest Elementalist. I'd like to be the first to invite you to study at Avalon Academy of the Arcane." She extended her hand out to Abigail. "How would you like to learn how to use magic?"

AVALON ACADEMY #2

Tea Time

Garrett

"So, I tried again, and I just couldn't connect with the Fulcrum, it was like it was someone else's." Lucas said, talking about class from earlier in the day.

Garrett Grant sighed and shrugged. "I guess you'll just have to keep practicing."

"Practice? Come now, you really think that's what I need? If I practice that just leaves less time for other things. Things th..." Lucas kept speaking, but Garrett's attention had drifted away from the unstoppable hurricane that was Lucas's style of one-sided conversation.

His eyes fixed on her again, the waitress who had served the tea Lucas and he shared. She was talking with a pair of academy professors, taking their orders presumably. The two of them chuckled, perhaps having told a joke, and she giggled along. By the three, even in the subdued candlelight, her smile was truly magnificent. Then she left, weaving her way through the tables past his own like a dancer tiptoeing her way across a stage. Her black and white dress, and pristine white apron rippled as she moved. As she passed, the scents of vanilla and lavender filled his nostrils, mixing with the aroma of the earl grey before him. He grinned dumbly, watching as she slipped behind the counter where all manner of tea, coffee, and other beverage making apparatus could be seen.

"...ey what are you smiling about? S'matter with you? Think it's funny that I lost my pet hamster?" He heard.

Then Garrett snapped his attention back to Lucas. "Oh, I, uh... well no, that's horrible."

"Forget about it, it happened ten years ago anyway. But you," Lucas pointed an accusatory finger, his bushy brown eyebrows lowering as he narrowed his hazel eyes. "You were watching her again, weren't you?"

He looked back over his shoulder, catching a glimpse of her as her deft hands carefully placed just the right amount of tea leaves in the fine teapot in front of her on the counter. "Who wouldn't?"

"Jesus, man. You watch her in class, you watch her here, hell, the whole reason we come here after class is because she works here in the first place. Why don't you just ask Tabitha out already?" Lucas said, taking a sip of tea. His lips curled in disgust.

"Oh... But I..." Garrett shook his head. "No. Just no, Lucas. She wouldn't want to go out with someone like me."

"Gary, you better do something. I mean, geez, what the hell is this stuff anyway?" Lucas said, sniffing the tea disapprovingly.

"Earl grey, her favorite. She lets it steep longer than normal to bring out the exact flavor she's looking for." Garrett said, watching Tabitha set a full tea set on a silver tray. She had a way of placing things that just felt... so right. Like that was exactly where it should have always been.

Lucas scoffed. "Well, it tastes like I'm eating a flower with a side of grass clippings. Why can't we drink coffee?"

"She doesn't like coffee..."

"Great for her. I like coffee. You like coffee. We should drink coffee." Lucas said. He could hear him take another sip.

She put a plate of tea cakes on the tray, along with a cream and sugar cup.

"Gary, damn it, look at me." And Garrett did so, finding Lucas a bit more red in the face than usual. "Buddy, I'm not coming anymore if you don't do something. This is sad to watch. The least you could do is man up and ask the girl." He gestured wildly, hands over his heart. "Take pity on me, Gary. Do it for me. I just can't watch this anymore.

And then her sweet, sing-song voice rang in his ears. "Did you need something?"

Garrett looked up, and there she was. Smooth, pale skin, large dark brown eyes, and long blonde hair held up in a bun. A loose curly lock of hair framed the left side of her face. She held the tray she had set up at the counter by the handles on either side. She was looking to Lucas, his waving and flailing must have caught her attention.

He smirked mischievously to Garrett, and then looked to Tabitha. "Oh, dear, not me. But, my best bud Gary really needed to say something."

Garrett's heart plummeted. He could feel the blood in his veins turn to ice as that wonderful face turned his way, her eyebrows raised expectantly. His mouth made half-noises and sputtered, completely unhelpful in the light of her eyes. All he could really manage was to smile, and raise his teacup.

"Are you trying to say you like it?" she said, tilting her head to the side. That stray lock of hair swung out free in the open, tense air without a care in the world.

He nervously nodded. His vocal cords had apparently decided to rebel against him, disobeying any demands he made. Though, his jaw and lips were not much better.

She beamed, and what a glorious smile it was. "Thank you! Just let me know if you'd like more! I'd be more than happy to brew some more!" And then she was off, weaving her way through the crowded café.

"Jesus Christ, Gary. I think that was the most painful, awkward thing I've ever seen in life," Lucas said, setting his cup down. "You are hopeless. I don't say that about anyone, but geez, if anyone is, it is you. You can't even talk to the broad."

"Don't talk about her like that. She's a goddess." Garrett said, perhaps too sharply.

Lucas held up his hands. "I surrender. No need to threaten me with a teacup, of all things." Garrett hadn't noticed he had pointed the delicate cup towards the Brooklyn native. "Look. If all you do is watch her, how are you going to get to know her?"

"I know a lot about her. She's in the top ten of our class, her favorite food is—" Garrett started.

"Buddy, this isn't no questionnaire. No pop quiz," Lucas interrupted, "Sure you might know some facts about her, but you don't know *why*. Why does she like what she likes? Hell, do you even know why she works here?"

Garrett looked down at his teacup, watching the brown, mirror like surface of the tea reflect his face.

"I think I've made my point." Lucas said, as he got up from his plush leather armchair.

"Where are you going?"

Lucas chuckled. "I'm going home, Gary. You should too, if you are just gonna stay here and stare at the poor girl like a creep. I'll see you tomorrow.

Garrett waved a goodbye, watching his friend leave through the stained glass front door. He scanned the café for Tabitha, but couldn't see her. Perhaps she had gone in the back to take a break.

Lucas was right. He had tried to talk to her multiple times, but he always froze around her, too afraid he would say something wrong. Who was he kidding? Everything he ever said was wrong. He took another sip of tea, but even it's soothing warmth and aroma wasn't enough to make it any less true.

And then, the most miraculous thing happened. From seemingly nowhere, an angelic figure came to sit at the armchair Lucas had sat in, and set her apron down at the table between them.

It was Tabitha. As their eyes met, she smiled, and said "Do you mind if I keep you company while I take a break?"

AVALON ACADEMY #3

Welcome Home

Abigail

Lauren led Abby to a large wooden building at the other side of the campus, which sat on a grassy hill that overlooked the rest of what might as well have been a small city. A lithe young woman hung up what looked to be bed sheets at a row of clotheslines off to the side. An impeccably maintained garden framed the border of the area, and wrapped around to the front of the building. Dozens of different kinds of flowers flooded the stretch, but Abby really didn't know the names of any of them. The symphony of scents carried from the flowers to her nose immediately set her at ease.

"Willa, dear, how are you?" Lauren said, curly copper hair loosely telegraphing the breeze.

"I know ye aren't bringin' another stray cat ta me. Yer lastun nearly burned 'is room, an' 'imself down," Willa said, in a rapid accent Abby guessed was Scottish or Irish, without turning around to face them. She kept going about hanging up the sheets. Abby was amazed at the speed the woman was able to work, barely able to keep up with her hands as she whipped the sheets from a basket, cast them across the waiting line, and then pinned them into place with clips she appeared to keep in her stark, straight black hair. She was tall, maybe a head or so more than Abby, and looked to be in her early twenties, but Abby couldn't be sure.

"Abigail, I'd like to introduce you to Willa Anderson. She's a Keeper here at the Academy for Elementalists. They take care of housing, food, and other necessities for our students who live at the Academy, rather than commute." Headmistress Corvinus, as Abby had learned she should call Lauren, said.

"Wait, live here? You mean I can stay here?!" Abigail didn't even try to hide the excitement in her voice.

The Headmistress smiled that same comforting smile. "Surely you didn't think we'd have you living on the streets? How would you be able to focus on your studies without a sound roof over head, and a full stomach?"

As if on cue, Abby's stomach audibly growled, causing her to blush in embarrassment.

Suddenly, Willa stood next to Abby, bright green eyes examining her closely. "Oh, poor dear. When last did ye eat?"

Abby smiled weakly "Yesterday morning, I think?"

"You think? Three keep me!" Willa sighed and shook her head, then pointed to the Headmistress. "You an' I will handle the I's and T's later." She looked back to Abby and pulled her towards the building's front door. "Right now, let's get ye fed an' cleaned up. Where did Lauren find ye, a trash heap? 'fraid them rags are a lost cause. Well get ye set in somethin' decent."

Like a loose leaf tossed about in a storm, Abby was pushed and pulled around the halls of the building. The walls and doors around her whipped past as the tempest of a woman swept her in a furious cyclone. Abruptly, she was stripped of her clothes, and thrown in a large bathing chamber. She yelped in surprise, feeling helplessly exposed.

"Oh, t'won't bite ye. That spring has been washin' sore an' tired bodies for millennia. Wash up with 'em buckets there an' soak. Just relax for a spot, an' I'll be back." Willa said. Abby turned her head around to say thank you, but by the time she did, Willa was already bounding through the door to the chamber. She was amazed by the speed and purpose with which the woman could move. She found herself somewhat unconvinced that humans *could* move like that.

Through the blanket of steam that filled the room, the chamber looked to be divided into two sections, one with stools and buckets, and the other half with a large pool. A communal bath of sorts? It looked as though she was alone, which somewhat set her at ease. Even thinking about someone seeing her like this, so vulnerable and uncertain, made her cheeks burn.

She saw what looked to be a fogged-up mirror next to her and wiped some of the condensation from the cool surface. A wretched, soiled face looked back at her. Its features were unfamiliar at first, but then she depressingly admitted that it was her own face. Those plain brown eyes were definitely hers, as was that mess of tangled black hair. It had been probably a month since she had been able to bathe, even longer since she had seen herself in a mirror. She nodded to herself, setting her mind to the task at hand. Where she came from, if you had a chance to bathe, you took it. Usually, though, she'd have a knife or something to chase off... others. But that had been whisked away with her clothes.

She washed away much of the caked-on dirt and grime with a bucket of water from the pool. Well, one was far from enough, it probably took at least seven to clear away the worst of it. A bar of soap she found helped clear her poor skin of even more, and even help her hair start to feel, well, like hair again.

As clean as she could manage, she dipped her scrawny body into the pool. The water was impressively warm, cutting through her skin to soothe her aches. A ledge in the wall allowed her to sit in the pool with the water coming up to her chin. She sighed in relief as she laid her head back on the smooth stone wall that held the water in.

For the first time since... well a long time, she actually let herself relax. No cutthroats peeking at her from around the corner, plotting God knows what. No desperate creatures looking to steal away what little nothing she had. All that mattered in that moment was the warmth of the water. She felt much more exhausted than she would have expected, but it was probably just because she was hungry. Again, with almost uncanny timing, her stomach growled. It wasn't an unfamiliar sound to her.

After a while, she felt she had stayed in the pool for far too long, and she got out of the pool. As she got up, she saw what looked to be a pair of towels, and something else lay next to it, beside the door where she came into the chamber. She wrapped one around her body, and the other around her head, and then examined the other article. It looked to be some kind of robe. She didn't remember any of these sitting there before.

Suddenly Willa came bursting from the door, and started, obviously not expecting Abby to be out of the bath yet. "Three keep me, pet, suppose there were a lass under all that soot after all."

Abby blushed and lowered her eyes as Willa led her out of the bathing chamber to what must have been a dressing room of sorts. She hadn't noticed it before, though she hadn't been able to notice much of anything in the whirlwind that took her to the bathing chamber. Willa looked her over, muttering to herself.

"Miss Willa?" Abigail started.

Willa visibly flinched, waving in the air as though she were shooing away a fly in her face. "Just Willa, lass. Just Willa."

Abby nodded, hesitating as the other woman unwrapped the towel from around her head, and started carefully going through her hair with a comb. "Right, Willa... That pool, how is it heated?"

"That un's a natural 'ot spring, of course." Willa said.

"So, not with magic?"

Willa snorted. "Oh, no need. 'sides, using magic for somethin' like that t'would be a waste."

"A waste?" Abigail winced as the comb came to a stubborn tangle.

"Could do with a haircut, poor dear," she said, muttering to herself. "Magic is difficult, of course. Using magic for somethin' as frivolous as heating a bath is like baking an entire loaf of bread to only take a single bite."

"Really? I guess that makes sense..."

Willa kept working at Abby's hair while Abigail thought to herself. Though uneasy about being touched, she had to admit that feeling the other woman's skilled hands at work was rather comforting. Then something came to her.

"Willa, what did you mean by the Headmistress bringing you stray cats?" she asked.

She heard the other woman sigh, but she didn't stop her work. "Suppose I did say that. Lauren is..." Willa cleared her throat. "Well, she has a soft spot for the wayward, the abandoned, or those who 'ave nowhere else to turn. They probably remind her of herself, since she was once so lost herself. But, that's a story for her to tell, not me."

"I think I understand..." And Abby did. Something in the Headmistress's eyes lit up when she realized wasn't a student. Now that look was starting to make sense.

"Suffice it to say that she isn't the only one who only truly found herself when she came here." Willa said before falling silent.

After a long while of careful combing, Willa sighed and stepped away. "Done what I can for now. I'll have to give you a cut after you've had somethin' to eat. You'll have to live with short hair for a while, I'm afraid, pet."

After Willa had gotten Abigail in the robe, she led her to another part of the building, though this time at nearly normal human walking speed. They came to what must have been the kitchen. Smooth stone counters flanked a stove set, and an old brick oven. The opposite wall held a large fireplace with a lazily smoldering fire, as well as several shelves that held plates, pans, and various other instruments and utensils. A large pot sat at the stove, which

Willa dashed over to tend to, lifting the lid and stirring the contents with a large ladle.

Abby stood awkwardly in the door as her nose caught a wonderful array of scents, both familiar and far from. Her empty stomach roared in response, no longer content with simply growling. Whatever Willa was cooking smelled marvelous.

"Come sit, child," she said before grabbing a bowl, scooping out some of what appeared to be stew out of the pot, and placing the bowl on one of the tables with a single stool.

Abigail sat down and eagerly grabbed at the bowl, shoveling down the contents as fast as she could. Willa just watched, either in horror, or amazement, Abby couldn't say. She picked up the bowl, and licked it, trying to get every bit of the stew she possibly could, before setting the bowl down again. Then, as if finally catching up with her, the taste of the stew came to her in a rush. Beef and root vegetables danced about on her taste buds with an overwhelming wave of savory spices and salt proudly carrying the entire assembly of flavors. She couldn't even begin to try and describe it out loud. It easily had to be the most luxurious meal she had eaten since...

Willa just chuckled. Abby must have made some dumb expression when she finally was able to taste what she had so ravenously consumed. "Suppose you'd like more?"

"I can have more?"

"O' course you can, pet." At that, Willa grabbed the bowl and filled it again with stew, before handing it to Abby again.

"Where did the good Headmistress fish yet out of, anyway?" Willa asked as she put the lid back on the well-worn pot.

"Well," Abigail started, unsure of exactly what to say. "She didn't, I guess. Lau—I mean, Headmistress Corvinus found me this morning after I snuck in through a door a couple of students used."

Willa froze and turned her head around at a seemingly impossible angle. "Snuck in? Why not use your admission key?"

"I don't have one…" Abby said reluctantly.

"Ye…" Willa started. "Dinna 'ave a key?"

Abby just shook her head in response.

"The Three Goddess must have let ye in… but why?"

Abigail shrugged. "I don't really know; I don't even know who The Three are…"

"Dinnae know The Three? Child, do ye even know where ye are?"

Abby, again, just shook her head in response.

"Ye know nothin' of this place? Avalon, the Academy? Do ye even know about Magic?" Willa said, slipping over to Abby, an astonished look on her face.

"No, not really. Well, I've heard stories about Avalon, you know, King Arthur and all." Abby lowered her eyes, the intense, inquisitive look in Willa's eyes difficult for her to bear. "And Magic, well, I've never seen anything like what happened with that sphere. I've seen street 'magicians', but everyone knows they are fake."

Willa took a step back, dumbfounded, then locked eyes with Abby. "You used the sphere, did you? You passed the test? The first time you tried it?!"

"Right, yes. I could hardly believe my eyes." Abigail cocked her head to the side. "Why? Doesn't everyone?"

"By the Three…" Willa breathed, a look of utter bewilderment on her pale porcelain features. "No wonder you asked how the spring was heated. All of it is new to ye"

She then locked eyes with Abby. "Listen, child. This place, all of it, is a place of learning about the Arcane, the powers that make up the universe."

"Like science?"

Willa shook her head. "Science only investigates and explains what it can see and touch. Magic is something deeper, something that cannae be explained, only understood, the hidden threads that hold our world together, and shaped her in her earliest days. Magic is everythin', and nothin', and all living things have a connection to it."

"All living things?" Abby asked.

"O' course. Everythin' in existence is connected to magic, but life 'as a special relationship with magic. It can shape magic in advantageous ways. It is how so many creatures are capable of otherwise inexplicable feats an' abilities."

Abigail thought for a moment, then asked, "So if living things can use magic... why don't people? Why doesn't everyone use it?"

"Some do and will never realize it. They put a kind of pressure on their environment, but it is so subtle so as to be unnoticeable, or cause them exhaustion." Willa then came to sit at the table with Abby, pulling up a stool from some unseen corner. "But most just aren't aware and may never be. We call them Latent. Few others choose not to use, or to forget magic. They are usually referred to as Recused."

"Choose? Why would someone choose something like that?"

Willa smiled weakly. "'fraid I dinnae understand it myself, dear."

Abby considered what she had heard. It seemed so simple now. "So, most people will never realize their connection... is it kind of like how people can have talents they never knew? How some people are naturals at playing an instrument, or something like that?"

"A keen 'un, aren't you, pet?" Willa smirked and nodded. "If'n you've never tried somethin', you'll never know if you 'ave an affinity with it. Most people will never *see* real magic, at least in a way they could understand it, so they will never 'ave that push to try an' tap into it themselves. It also dinnae help that magic is incredibly difficult to use and control."

"But some can without even knowing they can?" Abby asked.

"Exactly right. Some have a natural, reflexive, instinctive control that is usually awakened by some kind of traumatic event, or from a transcendent level of mastery of a craft or skill. We call 'em Reflexives. In fact, the first magic users were metal workers who started to realize they could control their forges and without even touchin' 'em, pushin' 'em hotter and burnin' longer 'an they'd be able to do normally. Eventually that reflexive control became somethin' they were conscious of, and they eventually were called here." Willa gestured around with her arms. "We call it Avalon now, but it has had countless names throughout the ages. I'm sure you've heard the name Atlantis, or some other lost continent or island."

Abby nodded her head, deep in thought about what she had heard. Somehow none of this truly surprised her. It just seemed to make sense. She hadn't known she could do what she did with the sphere until she had done it. Which made her think of another question. "Why are you surprised about me passing the sphere test?"

Willa's eyes snapped back to Abigail, they were harder again. A bit of that disbelief painted on her face. "Child, very, very few pass that test on their first attempt. In fact, I believe the last 'un who did was Headmistress Corvinus herself. Most study for at least a year, some even more'n that, practicing with a sphere before they pass."

"What does the test mean? Why is it special?" Abby asked.

"The test determines your future at the Academy. Ye see, not all students learn the same way, or can do the same things. There's three major kinds of magic, which some call Affinities, and each needs a very different approach to teaching. This divides the academy into Factions made up of those with similar affinities. Ye must have tested as an Elementalist, if'n ye are here and Lauren brought you." Willa suddenly shook her head, as if snapped out of a trance. "But enough of that, dear. Ye need to eat, then we'll see about what room to put ye in."

Abby grabbed at the bowl of stew, now likely cold, before hesitating. "Is… is it really alright for me to have this, any of this?"

Willa looked as though she had been struck. "Why would it not be, pet?"

"It's just…" suddenly Abby's vision grew blurry, tears welling up as her cheeks flushed hot in embarrassment. She lowered her eyes to the table.

And then she felt a pair of arms wrap around her. "Oh lass, life hasn't been kind to ye has it?" Willa whispered as she tightened her embrace.

Abigail could only shake her head in response.

"That ends today. Ye are under my care now." Willa said softly.

With that, Abigail couldn't stop herself from crying. It all seemed too good to be true. She was sure that she'd wake up, and be right back in the same slum, begging for scraps, and fighting to keep the others from taking what little nothing she had. The other woman gently rubbed her back as she sobbed, murmuring "there, there now."

As she slowly regained her composure, the older woman turned Abby's face to look at her. "We'll talk about everythin' later. For now, eat as much as you'd like."

It was the most wonderful words Abby thought she'd ever heard.

DEFIANT HORIZON

Defiant Horizon is a Near Future, Alternate History Cyberpunk Adventure set in a world teetering on the edge of world war. As some discover that they have supernatural abilities, will they choose to use them for good, or their own selfish ends?

PROLOGUE

Darkness falls,
Again and again,
Felled by cruelty
Salvation denied.

My world grows cold
Seeing him drift,
Sink down,
Dive so far away.

Ten years ago
Above Core Island, Hashishima City, Hashishima
Sunday, August 9th, 2025

Amanda gripped the armrests of her shaking black leather seat as her mom's personal VTOL lifted off the penthouse landing pad, and started climbing into the air. Her heart seemed to plummet to the ground in contrast. G forces, while dampened by the craft's system, clawed at her nerves. It was silly to be scared of flying. She practically flew every day. But, she was anyway.

Her mom sat next to her, calmly examining her wrist console, probably looking at something from work. She looked over to the pilot in the front, well, all she could really see was his helmeted head. Then she looked back to her mother. "Um… Mom?" Amanda asked shakily.

She shook her head, "Sorry, sweetheart, not right now."

Amanda sighed. She wasn't sure what she expected. Her mom seemed particularly agitated when she came home from school. Maybe something had happened at work?

"Yes?" her mother said as she pulled an earbud from her console. She must have gotten a call. "I'm headed there now. I should be there when you land."

With the craft aloft, Amanda felt she could dare to look out of the window of the craft, and was greeted by a sight that was well worth the risk. The sparkling city of Hashishima lay below as the VTOL pulled further away from Marshall-Saito Tower. Countless skyscrapers formed a forest of human ambition and ingenuity that they coasted through at a rapid pace. The slowly retreating sun set the buildings aglow, just like the shimmering liquid gold ocean just beyond.

"I don't care what they think! It's only a month behind the development schedule. That's nothing compared to the impact that Defiance would have!" Her mom shouted, her raised voice catching Amanda's attention. She sighed, and wiped her forehead. Then continued in her normal speaking volume, "I'm... I'm sorry Shigure. I just don't understand how they don't get what we are working on. They really want to pull the plug after a temporary stock price dip? We are building the world's first space elevator, the first manned deep space FTL exploration ship, the next generation SK Reactor, three cities on the Moon, and one on Mars, and they think a fraction of a percent dip right now really matters? Between government funding, and projected sales alone, they really want to panic over one project falling behind schedule?!" she scoffed, "Well, Glen Amphetrion can go to hell. I don't care. I'd cut the entire R&D branch just to save Defiance."

Her mom kept talking, but Amanda's attention drifted back to the window. They were over the Saito Channel at that point, and then over the countless docks and warehouses of Port Island. She guessed that they were headed to the Spaceport, given that they were apparently going to meet with Shigure, and he usually stayed on the New British Union Space Station *Citadel*. Her mother hadn't said where they were going when they had jumped in the craft.

Over past Port Island she could see the new Link Island, where construction of the space elevator had started. They had been working on the titanic foundation for almost a year, casting the entire island out of Ultra Crete where there had been nothing before but shallow ocean.

Amanda decided to look over the poem she had been working on for English to kill some time. If they were headed to the Spaceport, they still had about fifteen or so minutes before they would arrive. She found that the most she could accomplish was rereading how far she had written a couple of times, and finally removing a comma she had deleted, added back in, and deleted again perhaps five times over. She was stuck, a stanza from really bringing the whole thing together. But, anything she started jotting down felt wrong. The assignment was due the next morning, so she had to put something there.

She sighed. It wasn't as if she was writing some definitive masterpiece. Amanda knew she was probably taking the poetry assignment much too seriously. But, she liked writing, even if poetry wasn't her first choice. She just wanted to do her best to show her vision. That vision felt important. A lone figure, holding a handful of ashes, staring at a sunset on the horizon, hoping to see the sun rise again the next day. But, why? Why would there be doubt if the sun would rise again…?

The VTOL seemed to be slowing down. She heard the pilot say "Copy, Tower. Final approach vector Echo Mike Miner to Pad Charlie Three-Seven. Descending now." Amanda looked out of her window, and, sure enough, she could see the landing pad, subdivided into about a hundred plots, for atmospheric craft at the Amphetrion Spaceport. Just beyond the expansive landing pad, she could see the 33 metallic towers that made up the spaceport. They stretched for several miles, each the height of a skyscraper. Ships of all sizes could land at these towers, though the larger, half-mile long military ships had to use the 10 massive towers at the other end of the spaceport. The other 23, while shorter, still had to be 100 stories tall.

In a matter of minutes, the craft settled on the pad, and the doors slid open. Her mom stepped out first, placing her earbud back in her wrist console's casing. She must have finally gotten off her call. The thin, elegant, middle-aged woman ducked her head under one of the craft's Gravity Trauns, a metallic spear held by a short wing on either side of the fuselage, that gently, rhythmically hummed and crackled with energy in their idle state. Amanda, who wasn't as tall as her mother, had to duck her head as well, though only with a tilt to the side. She wasn't sure how they worked, but it had something to do with manipulating the force of gravity to provide propulsion. Next year in Sophomore level Science, she would learn about Gravity Trauns, Solon-Kaku Reactors, Lux Excedo Drive, and many other technologies that made the modern world possible. She knew this because her mother had written the curriculum for the high school science and mathematics program for the Hashishima school system.

A large man in a black suit greeted her mom. "Good evening Mrs. Marshall, Mr. Saito's shuttle will be landing in approximately 5 minutes"

"It's Ms., not Mrs.," she said in reply.

"My apologies, Ms. M—"

"Forget about it. Which tower is the reentry shuttle touching down at?" her mom asked They kept talking for a moment before starting to walk towards one of the landing towers. Amanda couldn't quite hear what they said over the low thumping sound of a neighboring VTOL ship taking off from the landing pad, gravity trauns glowing a bright teal as they surged with energy.

Amanda, following shortly behind, could tell from the tone in her voice that her mom was quite agitated, she had been since

Amanda had got home from school. Between this, and Shigure coming to meet *in person*, something serious had to be wrong. Now she wished she had paid better attention to what her mother was saying in the VTOL.

They came to Tower 4, and stepped into a large elevator that rocketed them to the top. Amanda had been to one of these before, several times, in fact, on one of their various trips to a space station, or one of the lunar colonies that were under construction. Her mom had promised they would go make a progress visit to Ares 1 on Mars in Spring. However, the sight never failed to amaze her. They stood on a large platform with a second level that was made of catwalks and storage for various equipment. Three large mechanical arms reached upwards from there, and then stretched outward. She could see the other towers, some with ships clutched by the landing arms, others vacant. Past there, she could see the city skyline to the North across Central Bay. The city, and all of its noise, worries, and neon glare seemed so distant from here, without being out of touch. The sun was maybe thirty minutes from fully setting in the clear, cloudless horizon.

The tower's PA system chimed, then a smooth male voice said "Apollo Astravia Flight 44 is on final approach. Prepare for docking procedure."

Amanda looked back up, and saw a glittering speck that quickly approached, resolving into a smooth, streamlined, arrowhead-shaped vessel. It looked to be plummeting towards the tower till a teal light flashed on the other side, and it began to slow. Likely a couple miles away in the air, she could hear the throbbing hum of the ships gravity trauns cutting the ship's momentum. By the time it came to settle in on the landing arms, it was practically stopped in the air. A klaxon rang as the ship made contact. The arms gingerly brought the ship down beside the tower, hydraulics whining against the strain, till, with a loud locking clack, they came to rest.

The dorsal half of the ship was a near pristine white in

comparison to the scorched black ventral half that served as a heat shield in case the ship's barrier failed in reentry. A panel near the bridge of the vessel hissed, then flipped open, revealing the entry hatch. A covered metal bridge from the tower slid out and clicked into place in the opening the panel had left. A notification tone chimed from the PA system, and the same voice announced. "Apollo Astravia Flight 44 has landed, passenger disembark and cargo unloading will now commence."

At that, the hatch twisted open, and after a short pause, people began stepping off the ship, and crossing the bridge onto the tower. The unmistakable silhouette of Shigure Saito was the first person to step off of the bridge. He was about Abby's height, and was an impressive barrel of a man. He looked to be just as formidable as the bodyguard who had met them when they landed, even if he was a good head and a half shorter. A warm smile swept his face, and he spoke in a gravelly voice, worn and beaten after decades of yelling in heated meetings, "You didn't tell me I'd get to see little Ami-chan too. Look at you. How old are you now? 16?"

Amanda laughed, and grinned back. "Just 15, Uncle Shigi," she said as she came in for a hug. He hugged her back tightly.

"Oh Ami, to think I held you on your first day of life. How small you were back then. To see you now, almost a woman. Gods, I truly must be an old man." Shigure said to her as they broke the embrace.

"Oh, Shigure, you were old when you met me as a fresh grad from Blue Spire." Her mom said.

Shigure grasped at his chest, as if he had been punched. "You wound me, Diana. After I came all this way."

"Oh, sure, like that could get to you after, what, ten divorces? Is that really the worst thing that's been said about you?" her mom said, a playful smirk on her lips.

"Ah, 13, actually. Last one didn't even last a month," Shigure said, shrugging with a sheepish grin.

Her mom laughed, shaking her head. A tense pause set in between them as they fell silent. Amanda wanted to say something, but nothing quite felt right.

"How bad is this, Shigure?" Her mom asked.

His eyes said enough before he even replied. "Amphetrion is threatening to force a vote to push you out."

"And wherever he leads, Mink, Farrow, and Takahashi follow... betrayed by Amphetrion of all people... He was our first investor, and now it's come to this..." Her mother ran a hand through her honey blonde hair, growling in frustration as she stepped away.

Shigure looked down, then back to her. "The investors are worried that you are too attached to the project to make sound business decisions."

"That's a load of shit and they know it." Amanda's mom snapped. She turned back around, pointing a finger. Anger had twisted her elegant features, fire burning in her light brown eyes. "You know how important this is. You know what this means! Why don't you just tell them? Make them understand!"

"I will, but you have to let me handle this. I think... you should visit the development team." Shigure said quietly.

Her mother looked confused. "But they're on Luna 3 why wo—" Then, realization fell into place, and she nodded. She said her next words in a resigned tone. "How long?"

"A week, maybe two. I can get this all to blow over, throw them a bone, make them feel like they won something. But they are agitated with you right now. Give them some space, and they'll forget all about this hiccup. It'll be back to business as usual. In the meantime, you going to see the team shows our direct support for the project, and an initiative to get it back on track." Shigure said. Amanda had never seen this side of the man. His voice was so... cold, calculating. She'd always seen the jolly, if short-tempered businessman. This was something different.

"When do I leave?" Her mother's eyes were hard. Amanda got the impression that this was almost like a parent giving orders to a child. She might have scoffed and fought at first, but she knew this wasn't a request. Amanda's brow furrowed in surprise and confusion. Was this how they really acted when she wasn't around? Her mom was *the* Diana Marshall: an unstoppable genius who was building revolutionary machines in middle school. Yet here was a deference she had never seen in her with anyone else.

Shigure looked down, and tapped something on his wrist console, then flicked it in her mother's direction. "I've got you booked on this flight back up to Citadel. You should be able to take the next Tsukuyomi flight from there."

Her mother looked away. "Always prepared, huh?" she scoffed.

"Diana, if there was another way, I'd have already—"

"Save it. I know." Her mother sighed. Shigure nodded in understanding.

"Can I come?" Amanda asked.

Her mom jumped like she hadn't know someone was behind her. She looked back with an almost terrified expression. "I—don't—"

"Actually, Diana, why not? I'm sure there's—"

"No," her mother said quietly, then much louder, "Amy... it just isn't a good time. You've got school, an—"

"I can just remote in like I did during the trip to London. It's not a big deal." Amanda crossed her arms and narrowed her eyes. She could tell how conflicted her mom was. If she could just...

Then she shook her head. "I don't think you understand how tense things are right now. This is a really bad—"

"Bad time, sure. Mom, I've been standing here listening the whole time. I'm not deaf. I want to—"

"The answer is *no*, and that's final," her mother snapped. Amanda, and even Shigure recoiled at the forcefulness of her voice.

Her mother's tense shoulders immediately sunk. She could tell her mom regretted what she said, or how she said it, but Amanda wasn't going to let her off easy. "Fine. Run away, just like Dad. What do I care?"

"Amy, ple—"

"You've made your choice. You've always told me that once you've made a decision, you follow through on it till you see it done." Amanda turned and took a couple steps away from the two. "Go. That's all there is to it. I'll be fine on my own."

Her mother's eyes lingered on Amanda for a moment, steeped in regret. Shigure said something Amanda couldn't hear, which her mother turned to reply to. They spoke for a few more minutes just out of earshot.

Amanda looked away, trying to calm herself down, and watched as various drones swarmed around the reentry ship Shigure had come in on. They were maintenance craft, checking for imperfections in the hull and flight systems. She recognized it as a Marshall-Saito Comet series shuttle. It was just one of hundreds, thousands of designs her mother had made personally. "Diana Marshall, the Goddess Creating the Future" as the Hashishima Report had described her once. Even goddesses had their flaws.

The PA system chimed a sharp tone, and then the voice came back "Boarding is now available for Apollo Astravia Flight 87 to NBUSS Citadel. All passengers please board. The flight will be lifting off in five minutes."

Her mother came and held her by the shoulders. "Amy, I'll be back soon, I promise."

Amanda could see tears welling in her mother's eyes, something that shocked her. She had never seen her mom cry, even that time when she had dislocated her shoulder. Her heart quaked in her chest. Amanda nodded, feeling tears involuntarily budding in her eyes as well. Her throat was too tight to say anything.

Her mother smiled weakly, and removed her necklace with a silver crescent moon pendant, and placed it in Amanda's right hand. "Have I ever not come back for this?"

Amanda shook her head. It was taking everything she had not to burst into tears.

She felt her mother's warm lips touch her forehead, and a pair of strong arms come around her in embrace. Amanda hugged back. Suddenly all of her anger and confusion seemed to be irrelevant. She whispered, "I love you."

Her mom whispered back "I love you too. Don't burn the house down while I'm gone."

"No promises," Amanda said with a smirk.

The PA system chimed again with a reminder for passengers to board, and the two broke their embrace. Her mother walked up to Shigure, said something for a moment, to which he nodded in response, and she continued on across the bridge to the ship. Once at the hatch. She showed a flight attendant her wrist console, and she was welcomed inside.

Amanda walked over next to Shigure, who put a comforting hand on her shoulder. "You know she didn't want to go."

"She's going, that's all there is to it..." Amanda said, somewhat surprised at her words.

She could hear Shigure sigh. He spoke in a subdued, reluctant tone. "I just hope you will understand one day."

They watched as maybe three dozen or so people walked aboard the ship. A final boarding notification rang out, bringing a handful more. Then the hatch spun closed.

A klaxon wailed, and the bridge to the ship slid back into the tower. The arms brought the ship up as the gravity trauns flared into life, their teal glow slightly warping the air around them. The arms let go of the ship, and it effortlessly floated into the air on its own.

Amanda watched as the ship hurtled further up into the sky. The sky was dark, the sun barely a sliver on the horizon, but its light was enough to shine on the metallic hull of the ship. She saw the ship lurch to the side. She'd never seen… it didn't look to be gaining altitude anymore. What was happening?

Suddenly, an explosion ripped through the ship, cleaving the sleek arrowhead in two, before the two halves were consumed in a massive burst of blue-white fire, and a visible ripple of force. Stunned for an instant, Amanda screamed at the sight, bringing her hands to her mouth.

She tried to call for her mom, but the concussive burst drowned her out, and she was thrown to the platform's floor. A wave of heat ripped past her, like a rush of steam from a piping hot oven. The sound of continuing sympathetic detonations clawed at her ears.

Amanda felt something come over her, and she looked up to see Shigure hunched over her. He shouted into her ear over the deafening cacophony. "JUST STAY DOWN, I'LL KEEP YOU SAFE!"

Over his shoulder, she could see debris raining down from the explosion, bits of metal, glass, and… bodies… Plummeting back to the ground.

Amanda felt her vision begin to fade. Before she closed her eyes, she saw a dark figure with bright white tails streak across the sky.

DEFIANT HORIZON #1

Code 50

A thousand little threads,
Creased by time.
We are all the sum
Of what we survive.
Good deeds and crimes.

Tachibanaya, Hashishima City, Hashishima,
Wednesday, August 8th, 2035

"Overwatch, 2319 with that Delta 1. We're Code 12. En route to HQ." Monica heard over her Hashishima Police Force dispatch AI radio connection. She sat in the lovely, cozy interior of Tachibanaya, her favorite coffee shop on the outskirts of town. It had been remarkably quiet on the dispatch radio tonight. A few drunk drivers, a couple domestic calls, the usual stuff, but not as much as she'd expect. She'd been listening pretty much all day as she combed through news reports, and Current, on her holo console. She had about a dozen holopanels up with various programs and feeds running. Her dark brown eyes darted between them, taking in the information, eliminating garbage data, and filing away useful points nearly as quickly as they appeared.

There had been three sightings of the Kuroi Kitsune just this week, but it looked as though there were no new sightings last night. She had killed a lower-level drug dealer, three suspected hit men for the Kuznetsovs, and the head of a human trafficking ring this week. Well, it was assumed that she killed them. The marks made by presumably white-hot claws, and plasma bursts all but confirmed they were her victims. There had been copycats of the Kitsune over the years, but something was always off on the details. No, these were definitely Kitsune strikes, and just showed that the frequency of her attacks was further increasing. What once was a perhaps monthly, or even quarterly occurrence had accelerated to multiple times a week in the span of just a year. Sure, criminal activity had similarly increased, but there had to be more to it than that. Something was happening, and she needed to find out what. She needed to find *her*. She stared at that same picture a Current user had posted when they had caught the Kitsune leap across Ford Plaza this week. A dark figure with nine glowing tails streaking behind her.

Frustrated, she swiped the news feeds away and brought up the code interface for her latest pet project. She wasn't satisfied with the news and social media aggregator bot she had programmed. It seemed to pull too many irrelevant stories or miss things in social media posts because of bad spelling, or conflicting factors. She needed to retrain the algorithm that helped it judge what was useful. Monica took the archive of articles and posts she had collected over the years on the Kitsune and had her data model AI start working on modeling, testing, and corrections for her to review later. The better results she got from the aggregator, the less time she wasted with false positives and irrelevant data. She'd had enough when the aggregator had started pulling memes about the Kitsune as actual news. This time she'd written code to help mitigate pulling outright troll and joke posts on Current, letting the bot examine the user's post history to judge whether the user met a certain trust threshold. The more obviously fake posts, or memes, the lower the score. She'd see if that helped.

Haruka, the shops owner's daughter came to her with a plain white mug, and a small plate that held a gorgeous muffin. "You know, if you keep working on your days off, your Captain is going to have a fit again, Lieutenant Ichinose." She said as she set the coffee and muffin before Monica.

Monica twitched, the title making her cringe. "Haru, really, just call me Monica."

"I can't help that I'm still excited about your promotion to Lieutenant, The youngest in Hashishima Police Force history at that." Haruka said with a grin.

"Oh, come now, that was a year ago," Monica groaned. She took a sip from the mug. As always, the dark, rich, and complex House Blend was exactly what she needed to feel herself again. She still couldn't get Keiko to tell her the blend of beans she used. The notes of brown sugar, chocolate, and sweet orange filled her soul as she took a second sip. Could she really blame Keiko for being tightlipped about the blend? If she had something this sensational, she'd take the secret to her grave.

Haruka sat down at the table with Monica, and sighed. Much like the dispatch radio, Tachibanaya was exceptionally quiet. There was Ravi over at the fireplace reading a book like usual. He was probably on his second cup of coffee, and his girlfriend should be showing up soon, but Monica couldn't remember her name. The inseparable pair of older women, Gertie and Lyanna were gossiping about work, or so she had overheard. Apparently, Frank in Accounting was sleeping with Beth, again.

Otherwise, most of the dark oak tables were vacant, the eclectic collection of books and curios on the shelves that surrounded the space were untouched, and just Haruka worked behind the counter. Most of the regulars for a Wednesday night were total no shows. Tachibanaya was by no means a massively popular establishment, but it was a hidden gem with a dedicated following among locals. It was rare to see it so empty, even late into the night. Its prime location right next to the main campus of Blue Spire University made it a choice spot for students to meet up, or to buckle down for an all-nighter. That's how she had found it herself. The massive, barrel-chested Carter usually would have gotten here thirty minutes ago with his friend Tanya to help her learn to play chess. Little did he know that Tanya was only learning chess to get close to him. Then again, maybe she had finally confessed and the two were on a date or something. That would be a welcome change.

"Overwatch, 0421 here. Have a Delta 1 on 6th and Carter. Black sedan. Forwarding information. Making contact now," she heard. Another drunk driver. Monica sighed, and took a bite of the cinnamon swirl muffin Haruka had brought. The rush of sugar and cinnamon was enough to put a smile on her face. "Haru, did you make these?"

Haruka chuckled. "Oh, Mama's been trying to teach me her recipe, but I just can't get the hang of baking. Too finicky."

"Can't say I blame you. If it doesn't come in a box, I'm hopeless," Monica said, taking another sip of coffee.

"Hey Monny?" Haruka probed.

Monica tilted her head to the side. "What is it?"

"Well, I mean, do you think she's real?" Haruka shook her head, blushing in embarrassment. "The Kuroi Kitsune. I know you're in the task force set up to find her. But, do you believe she's real?"

Monica smirked. "With the wealth of evidence linked to her, I think her existence is hardly a matter of faith, or belief. In fact, I think doubting her existence is a rather irrational position to have. Her victims are real, the sightings and firsthand accounts have been tested and verified dozens of times. It would make *less* sense for her not to be real."

Haruka seemed to think about it for a moment, and then asked, "So, do you think she's a spirit, or demon like the legends say?"

"Now that I can't really say. I'd have to meet her to start to answer that." Monica took another sip of coffee.

"Yeah, but do you think those kinds of things even exist?" Haruka asked.

Monica saw a cockpit in ruins, blood splattered all over the walls, the muzzle of a gun resting against her forehead, and... her... She shook her head to clear the memory away, then looked back to Haruka with a fake smile. "Now that, I *do* believe."

"How do you know?"

"A story for another time, Haru. Let's just say that I hope you don't have the same experience I did." Monica said, closely guarding her tone.

They sat in silence for a bit. Monica kept listening to the dispatch radio, but nothing out of the norm came up. After a bit, Haruka got up to check on Ravi, by the fireplace. She hadn't noticed it before, but she realized that he was reading a copy of *The Unionist Papers*, by Hamilton, Burns, and Jay. He must have been reading it for British History class. It felt like only yesterday that she had read it herself.

Almost unnaturally, Haruka appeared next to Monica as she finished her last bite of muffin. "Can I get you anything else?" she asked.

Monica shook her head and shrugged. "Nah, I'd better head back home."

"No hot date lined up?" Haruka said with a smirk.

"Gods no. Like I have time for that." Monica laughed half-heartedly as she stood up and swiped on her holo console to pay her bill, adding a tip that was twice what she owed.

Haruka put a slight hand on Monica's shoulder, and spoke softly, "You should make time. I just want you to be happy. You've been alone since the day I met you when you were a college student, and I was just some stupid kid."

"I am happy. And you were never stupid. Don't sell yourself short," Monica said, waving her hand in the air dismissively.

"Yeah right, if you hadn't tutored me, I'd have failed Algebra,

Coding, and Physics." Haruka countered. She picked up the cup and plate she had brought over with one hand and wiped the table off with a towel she kept on her apron with the other. Haruka always was a bit of a clean freak, which served her well working at the coffee shop, since it was always spotlessly clean. It hadn't always been, with her, at times… absent-minded mother.

Monica smiled warmly. "We all have different strengths, Haru, even if we don't know them yet. When I was your age, I found that out… the hard way." She looked away for a moment, then she closed her eyes, and put that smile back on for Haruka. "You'll see, some day. You have a good night, alright?"

"Of course, you know it's always a good night here," Haruka said with a smirk, and she set off to the counter with the dishes in her hands.

It was only a few strides to the glass front door. Monica took one last deep breath of the scents of fresh coffee and baked goods before stepping back out to the rest of the world.

The air was pleasantly warm, having cooled from the heat of the day. That humidity was still there, though. Between that, and the periodic dark clouds that loomed overhead, it certainly felt like rain was only moments away. But it had felt that way for three days now.

She turned down 4th Street. Her apartment was a few streets away, nothing too far for a short walk. These days, though, many would call for a car for a much shorter trip. She saw that as inefficient, a misuse of resources. Besides, walking back home from the coffee shop gave her time to think.

Captain Gambini had really tore into her yesterday after he had found out that she had worked 29 days in a row without taking a day off. She knew it had been too long since she hacked the timekeeping AI to alter its logs for her activity. She was getting sloppy again. If only he knew how long she really had been working without taking a day off… As a result, he had put her on mandatory leave for the rest of the week.

Thankfully, the security for the main server was pretty easy for her to work around, so she had full access to her virtual workstation, case files, and the dispatch radio. Even if she wasn't at the police station, she could still get things done. The captain's heart was in the right place, but she couldn't just take a day off. She might miss something important. She had to stay on the hunt no matter what.

Monica sighed. This wasn't what she wanted to think about. She needed to work on some new stimulus tests for Ay—

Suddenly, she heard the unmistakable chattering report of rapid gunfire, making her reflexively duck down into a crouch. It had to be perhaps a street or two away. She pulled her Bastion Arms Crossfire pistol, racked the slide as she got up from her position, and quickly moved towards the sound. More gunfire burst in the warm night air. It was a different caliber than the first, which was met with more rapid reports, and the sound of glass breaking.

She came to the corner of an office building at 3rd and Lake and peeked around the corner. Over on what she guessed was Kozuki Street she could see a large, armored truck that looked like a Razorback parked outside the Byakko office building. There were three people dressed in matching black body armor, with what appeared to be tactical helmets firing rifles into the building's lobby. A couple flashes, accompanied by the snap of handgun fire told her that the security inside the building must have been fighting back. Glass littered the concrete sidewalk and street in front of the entrance

Monica quickly switched the dispatch radio back on. "Overwatch, this is 1701. Code 50 in progress at 3rd and Kozuki, Byakko Building. At least three assailants. Long guns, looks like body armor too, plus one armored truck from what I can see. Shots fired. They're fighting with Byakko security. Can I get eyes on?"

The dispatch AI immediately responded, "Copy, Code 50 in

progress, repeat, Code 50 in progress. Shots have been fired. All available units please respond on private channel with location and ETA. 1701 please standby."

Monica nodded, taking a deep breath to steady herself. She tapped a button on her wristwatch to activate a holo display that formed over her left eye. It was a threat detector she had made a couple months ago, but hadn't had a chance to test. Peeking around the corner again, the lens of the detector drew a silhouette around the three behind the truck. It also provided analysis of their equipment that it was able to recognize. They had matching Defenstech Operator 7 body armor, and were using Shenlong Type 67 assault rifles. The truck was a Defenstech Razorback, like she thought. These guys had to be pros to field this kind of kit, or had deep pockets. She whispered after she switched off her microphone to the dispatch radio, "Ayaka, I need you to be my second set of eyes."

A light feminine voice responded in her right ear from the earpiece she wore, "Understood. Three targets have been detected. One is moving towards the building entrance"

Sure enough, one of the silhouettes was walking to the front door of the building, rifle raised. Green and purple neon light glared on his dark, armored bulk, as he neared the large holo sign with the tiger logo for Byakko Industries draped over the top of the building's threshold.

Ayaka then said. "The closest target currently has their back turned to you, and appears to be checking the other direction of the street. From this position you have a 87% chance to hit given your average accuracy statistics."

"Can my Crossfire penetrate that armor?" Monica asked.

"Analyzing. Defenstech Operator 7 body armor is rated to withstand shots from a 9.9mm pistol, however the Bastion Arms 9.9mm Lancer ammunition you have loaded should be able to penetrate with a direct hit. Chest shots are not advisable as that is where the most armor plating is located." It was amazing how quickly she could perform analysis now. All of that training had really paid off.

"Anything else you can tell me?" Monica asked anxiously. She was getting worried that she hadn't heard back from Overwatch yet.

"Based on acoustic analysis, and traffic camera data, I anticipate there are five enemy assailants. There have been shots from five distinct Shenlong rifles. It is possible there is another in a different location, or waiting in the car. The Defenstech Razorback has six seats. 65% confidence conjecture." Ayaka said.

Monica switched back to talking to the dispatch radio. "Overwatch, 1701, what's the story on those cameras?"

"Unable to access building surveillance at this time, nor any other data. The data lines may have been severed," Overwatch responded.

Monica rolled her eyes. Of course. If they had the surveillance feed, the attack would have been reported immediately as it happened. She should have anticipated that. "Copy Overwatch. How long until back up gets here?"

The dispatch AI then chimed, "1701, the closest unit is ten minutes away. Do not engage. You are ordered to observe only."

The gunfire back and forth continued as the dispatch AI spoke. Monica growled in frustration. "1701 here. That's not going to work. There're people in danger in there."

Overwatch responded coldly, "You are not authorized to take action at this time. You are currently on leave. Do not engage. Acknowledge this order."

"Screw that." She said back before she severed the connection. Monica tapped a button built into her holo console at the base of her neck, and the image of armor plating flashed onto her chest. She gave it a moment, and then knocked on it with her knuckles to check. Sure enough, the holo flash forge had worked. She just hoped she didn't have to see how *well* it had worked.

Monica peeked around the corner again, raised her pistol with both hands, lining up the faint holosight with the base of the neck of the closest target, and pulled the trigger. A bullet burst from her handgun, cutting through the air to meet its target. But, as she fired, the man turned, and the bullet tore into his right shoulder. The man yelped in pain, and she fired two more shots. One ricocheted off of his helmet, while the other hit it squarely, sending bits of dark composite flying in the neon light.

"Warning, second target is engaging." Ayaka said just as Monica saw the other man behind the truck turn to face her. She ducked behind the wall just as a spray of bullets peppered the spot. She heard a shout, but couldn't make out what the man said. He was most likely calling for help.

"Did you catch what he said?" Monica asked.

Ayaka responded immediately, "Unclear. I do not recognize the language, and he is just out of range of the microphone."

She needed to move. There were at least two attackers that she knew about for sure. If Ayaka was right there could be three more. They could be inside the building, waiting in the truck, or in another spot that Ayaka and Overwatch couldn't see with traffic or surveillance cameras. Her position was compromised, and if she didn't engage from another, they could figure out a way to flank her. As if reading her mind, Ayaka displayed a translucent map over her threat detector lens with a marker. "This position presents the best opportunity for successful re-engagement"

Without a second's hesitation, she broke into a full sprint around the building to a position that was right up against the Byakko building. But as she came around the corner to the alleyway she needed to cut through, a man in black armor opened fire from further back. Air rushed from her lungs as she felt two punches in the chest before she managed to scramble back around the corner. Chunks of 3d printed concrete brick and dust sputtered from the corner as bullets ripped into the wall.

Monica struggled to catch her breath. The shots had knocked the wind out of her, and her heart was pounding erratically. She felt at her chest armor with a shaking left hand, thankfully the flash forged armor had worked, though she wasn't keen to see how many more hits it could take. Almost to prove the point, the armor started to crumble, and she dismissed it with a tap to that same button she had used to summon it. The armor vanished into thin air as if it had never been there. It didn't seem as though she had been hit anywhere else. Monica had been incredibly lucky, but that luck would run out soon if she didn't do something.

The man who had shot her stopped firing, and she gambled on the hope that he was changing magazines. Using the threat detector's best estimate of his location to prepare herself, she whipped around the corner, lined up her shot, and squeezed the trigger twice as she aimed for the head. One bullet blasted through the neck, puffing out a cloud of red behind him. The other glanced harmlessly off the helmet.

That was two down, and she still didn't know for sure how many left. She didn't have time to guess as bullets came flying from where she had come from. Monica dove to the ground and cursed. A blue dumpster had blessedly been right behind her. Bullets rattled into the heavy steel bulk. She thought she could hear voices from around the corner where the guy she had just shot was. It could be more coming to flush her out.

A flash of white from over the dumpster caught her attention, and Monica heard a scream accompanied by some kind of hissing sound. She dared a peek over the dumpster... And standing over the mauled body of her attacker was a tall, sleek, feminine figure clad in almost alien black armor. Nine blazing white-hot tails of plasma flowed and coiled behind her. Claw-like gauntlets made up her hands, the claws also glowed white-hot, as if heated by plasma. On the head was a sleek helmet with three crown-like points, and a mirror-like circle in the middle about the size of Monica's hand.

It was her: the one who had slaughtered criminals for centuries, the one called a demon by some, and an angel to others. The legendary avenging spirit of Hashishima, the Kuroi Kitsune. Not a picture, not a story, not a historical account, not a meme, not some artist's rendering. It was really her.

The Kitsune looked from the man she had killed over to Monica, and tilted her head. Mesmerized, Monica realized that the mirror-like visor on the helmet didn't show her reflection. She was at a complete loss for words. For almost ten years she had looked for the Kuroi Kitsune, and there she stood…

Suddenly, the Kitsune leapt into the air, landing behind Monica. She whipped around to see the Kitsune pounce on another attacker, slashing into them with her claws. The scent of burning plastic and flesh shot through the air as a spray of bullets from an unseen attacker clattered against the Kitsune's armor. The tails whipped towards the new threat, and Monica looked around the corner just in time to see two of the ribbon-like tails slice the man in half.

And then she was gone, rocketing into the warm night air with a titanic jump. Monica fell to her knees, dumbfounded about what she had just seen. She had never doubted that the Kuroi Kitsune was real. Ten years of collecting records of sightings, surveillance footage, cases of her victims, even seeing many of them herself over the years had been more than enough to convince her that she was real. It would have made less sense for her to *not* exist. Something about seeing her right in front of her, though, made her feel… well she didn't know. The entire encounter felt as though it had been some kind of dream.

Droplets of water began plummeting to the ground. She looked down at her still shaking hands, precipitation budding on her icy skin The rain had finally come, and with it a VTOL unit touched down next to her. A squad of police in full tactical gear jumped out and surveyed the situation. She watched, as if from a great distance, them take positions, two charging down the alley towards where the truck had been, two running down Lake Street to where she had been, and three checking the bodies of the people around her.

"Lieutenant, are you hurt? Are you ok?" one of the officers, Curtis, said, a stunned look on his face as he looked her over. He took a knee in front of her, and checked for injuries.

It took her a moment to find the right words. "No... just sore..."

Another officer, who was standing over where the three men had been killed around the corner, looked back to her. It was Simmons. "What the hell happened, Monny?"

All she could manage was, "It was her."

DEFIANT HORIZON #2

Looking Forward

Circlets of golden destiny
Cast upon endless horizons
Stolen away, cast asunder.
Shall I rise,
An ill-fitting shadow,
To reclaim?
Can what is lost
Ever truly be found
Again?

Marshall Space Elevator Station, Link Island, Hashishima,
Thursday, August 9th, 2035

"My mother believed wholeheartedly in the promise of tomorrow. It was her belief that our greatest days, our greatest triumphs, were always just ahead. Diana Marshall came from nothing. She grew up on the streets of New York before the Revival. Her parents had nothing. She had nothing.

"But, she worked everyday to rise above where she came from. Diana cleaned houses, washed clothes and dishes, and did whatever else she could to make money to pay for school tuition up until she earned a full scholarship to Oxford. Once she graduated, she started working on technology that would change our world. *Hitobito* named her 'the most powerful, intelligent, and inventive person of the modern world.' The *New British Times* called her 'The Da Vinci of our Age.' Along with her business partner, Shigure Saito, she built Marshall-Saito Technologies, and got to work to make her dreams a reality.

"She made it her mission in life to bring a piece of tomorrow to today. Her work in city planning, advanced construction, and management made our beautiful city what it is today, a model gradually copied around the world. She personally designed the second generation Solon-Kaku Reactor, which revolutionized our energy future, making the experimental technology commercially viable at scale. Her interest in display technology gave us the holo computers we use today. Her collaboration with Gatesoft brought the promise of true artificial intelligence closer to reality than ever before.

"Later in her life, her interest began to turn to the stars. She told me that they were the only thing that kept her going when she felt like giving up when she was a kid. She wanted to bring us to those stars. While she didn't personally work on the Lux Excedo drive, she funded Dr. Cromwell's research into the engine that enables a ship to travel faster than the speed of light. Diana then lead development of mass production methods for the drive. She then helped design and develop the *NBUS Horizon,* the first starship that will carry mankind to another star system starting in just a few weeks.

"But she knew that our spacefaring future would be accelerated by a cheap, efficient, and reliable means of transporting goods and people to and from space. She believed that the backbone to that dream was a space elevator. This marvel of engineering can take someone to the cusp of the stars for a quarter of the cost as a ship, making space travel and commerce cheaper and more accessible for everyone.

"Today my mother's dream becomes a reality. I am incredibly

proud to announce the official opening of the Marshall Space Elevator. From this moment on, the stars are closer than ever before. Let us reach up towards the stars together." said Amanda Marshall. She stood at the massive east entrance to the Elevator. A wall of frosted glass doors sat behind her, nestled under a large marble archway. A massive crowd of people, and a box of press from all over the world cheered.

At last line of her speech, a chime rang, followed by a smooth masculine voice announcing, "The Marshall Space Elevator is now open. Welcome." And the glass doors swung open.

"Now go forth into new horizons," Amanda said before dismissing the holo microphone over her mouth. She stepped away from the doors, and through a narrow corridor her security detail had made through the crowd of spectators and people eager to be among the first to take the Space Elevator up. A joyous uproar surged as people flooded into the entrance behind her.

Batou walked in stride with her, sharp black eyes surveying the crowd as they walked away from the main elevator terminal. As usual, he had put himself between her and any perceived threat, in this case the large gathering of people. Her bodyguard, and personal assistant, spoke in a tense voice just loud enough for her to hear, "you did well, ma'am. Your mother would be proud."

"I'm sure she would be," Amanda said in reply. They made it to the VTOL pad, where her sleek silver Phoenix 7s craft sat, gravity trauns sparking in an idle spool.

She turned to look back at the Elevator Terminal one last time. The vast majority of the crowd had barely even made it to the doors into the titanic building, and they would be far from the last. Her mother's dream, this one at least, had come true. Amanda's eyes followed the black composite shaft from the top of the Terminal, and up as it reached even further than she could see into the clearing early morning sky. She said to herself, "One more down, Mom, right on schedule. The *Horizon* next."

Then she stepped into her VTOL craft. She settled into the pilot seat, the crash gel forming to her thin body as she pulled on her seat belts. An orange holo heads up display flared into life on the windshield. Just as she had completed preflight checks, Batou came to sit in the copilot seat. "All clear, ma'am."

"All Clear, Tower, Ready for launch," Amanda said.

"Copy, Marshall One, go for take off," the air traffic control AI responded after a moment.

Amanda grabbed the controls, and lifted the gravitation orb. She could feel the craft set off from the pad as the gravity trauns thrummed. Once she got the ship to a safe altitude, and locked it in, she turned the vector and attitude controls towards the city. She spared a glance for the massive hexagonal Elevator Terminal building as it passed from view. She could already see a fleet of freight VTOL ships come in for a landing at the commercial end of the building. Ten years... it felt like only yesterday she had seen the foundation poured.

"What do we know about the sighting last night?" Amanda asked, trying to pull her mind from the past.

Batou brought up a holo display. "Looks like a mercenary crew hit on Byakko. Unknown what they were after. An HPF officer intervened, and got in a firefight. Then the Kitsune dropped in, and finished the crew. The officer insists the Kitsune came to save her."

"Did this officer see it happen? Do we have a name?" Amanda looked over to Batou beside her.

"I took the liberty of talking with Chief of Police Collins this morning as you were preparing for your speech," he said with what passed for a smirk on his stern face. "The officer involved was Lieutenant Monica Ichinose. Special Crimes. She investigates incidents with the Kitsune, and other strange cases that don't fit in other task forces."

"I thought I recognized her name. We've bought her reports before, right?" Amanda said. They were just about to come over

Port Island as they spoke. To think that it used to be half the size it was today back on this same day ten years ago, when she was just a silly girl fussing over some stupid poem.

"Yes ma'am. Very... detailed." Batou said. He was reviewing something on his holo console.

"What is it?"

There was that shadow of a smirk again. "In consideration of your recent, very generous donation to the Hashishima Police Force Pension Fund, Chief Collins is willing to set up a meeting with Lieutenant Ichinose."

"Well, I always have tried to be generous to the people who keep us safe, haven't I? Well done." Amanda said, shaking her head with a laugh.

A short flight later, Amanda set the craft down on one of the Hashishima Police Force Headquarters landing pads. Chief of Police Eugene Collins was there *himself* to greet them in the blue and gold military-style uniform of the Hashishima Police Force. As she took off her helmet, and set the craft to idle, she asked, "Batou, just how much did I send?"

"500 million pounds, ma'am. Really quite generous of you." He replied.

"Generous, right." Amanda said, shaking her head in disbelief. If there was one thing Batou was particularly proficient at, it was getting people's attention, and not just with his striking physique.

They stepped out of the cockpit, and onto the rooftop landing pad. The headquarters was stouter than most of the neighboring skyscrapers, but was much wider to accommodate for a large landing pad for dozens of VTOL craft at once, and an internal hangar bay for even more vessels. This gave this gave Amanda the impression that the building was surrounded by impossibly tall walls of glass, steel, and neon lights. She had personally supervised the team that had designed the new Headquarters for the Bastion Defense Solutions when they took over the

Hashishima Policing and Security contract from Defenstech six years ago, so she was quite familiar with the building. This was, however her first time visiting since it's construction.

"Ms. Marshall, it is a honor to see you!" Chief Collins said. He was a portly man with wiry brown hair, and a face that always reminded Amanda of a bulldog. If she was honest, his grumbling voice that sounded as though his cheeks were stuffed with cottonballs only reinforced the impression.

She smiled and held out her hand as she stepped up to the man. He shook it eagerly. "Please, just Amanda is fine. My mother was Ms. Marshall."

"And what a remarkable woman she was. I regret not having known her personally. I was just a Sergeant back then." The Chief sighed. "My, how times change." He took her hand so that her arm hooked around his as he moved to escort her. The height difference between the two was almost comical as she had to lean over for her arm to be low enough for the gesture. She had, after all, inherited her mother's height in the end.

"My assistant says one of your officers saw the Kitsune last night?" Amanda asked.

Chief Collins seemed to hesitate for a moment. He kept a jovial expression, but she could tell the topic made him uneasy. "Ah, yes, Mr. Batou mentioned your interest in the case." They stepped onto an elevator with the black, white, blue, and gold logo of Bastion Defense Solutions, a black shield with three crossed swords, one white, one gold, and one blue.

"I hope there is no issue in meeting with the Lieutenant?"

"No issue, no. I just..." the Chief cleared his throat as he activated the elevator, and they started to descend. "I wonder why a young woman like yourself would be interested in such things. To be frank, I don't put much stock in the stories myself."

"Chief Collins, one of your officers says she had an encounter with the Kitsune herself, and you don't believe her?" Amanda asked.

"Lieutenant Ichinose is brilliant, too brilliant for her own good. Her supervisor just found out she had secretly been working for over a month without taking a day off, and he suspects that she's been working much, much longer than that. She is dedicated, if a bit... eccentric-- to say it politely." The Chief said.

Amanda's brown eyes narrowed. "You think she hallucinated the encounter? Made it up?"

"That's perhaps too strong a word. You see, she's been tasked with finding the Kitsune, and investigating cases that are possibly linked to her. She's been dedicated to that for quite some time, with little but conjecture to show for it." The lift came to a stop, and they walked down an austere polycrete hallway. "What are the chances that the day she is put on leave that she intervenes in an active shooter incident, and just so happens to have a direct encounter with the object of her work after all this time?"

"Or she was just in the right place at the right time. The Kitsune attacks criminals supposedly, so would her chances of encountering the Kitsune improve dramatically being at the site of an active crime?" Amanda offered. She had reclaimed her arm, and was relieved to stand up straight again as they stopped just before a large metal door.

Chief Collins nodded. "Possible, yes. But, in my experience, 'Right place at the right time' is quite often much too good to be true." He placed a hand on the door handle, and then hesitated. "A word of caution, if you will, Amanda."

"Go on."

"Lieutenant Ichinose has been working for God knows how long, continuously, and has just been through a firefight where she was very much so outnumbered, and very likely should be dead right now. This kind of stress can do things to memory, and the mind." He cleared his throat again. "Keep this in mind before jumping to conclusions about what she says."

"Believe me, I know a thing or two about stress." Amanda said, stepping closer to the door.

The Chief bowed his head. "Of course, Amanda." He turned the handle, and opened the heavy metal door for her. "Again, thank you so much for your incredible generosity!"

Amanda entered what appeared to be an interrogation room, not exactly what she had expected. It was a spartan, bare metal chamber with a table and four chairs in the middle. Seated in one of the chairs, with her back to the door, was a feminine figure with long, coarse, obsidian hair, who was typing away at a holo console. A black trench coat was draped across the back of the chair.

The woman had perhaps 10 or so holo screens up, displaying various information. One had what Amanda supposed was body camera footage of the Kitsune. Another showed a map of the intersection of 3rd Street and Kozuki Boulevard. Several color-coded markings had been made over it. Three had some kind of code interface, but she didn't recognize the language. One had pictures of maybe 5 men cycling. The rest of the screens she couldn't quite make out.

"Ayaka, any luck with the spectral analysis?" the woman said quietly. She seemed to be lost in thought, not even noticing Amanda and Batou had entered the room.

A soft feminine voice responded, "Inconclusive. Unable to determine the composition of the subject's armor"

"Why am I not surprised..." the woman said, running a hand through her luxuriously long hair. "Remind me to try a tungsten weave with the flash forge. Maybe that'll keep the armor from crumbling next time after the first hit."

"Noted, I'll have the fabrication algorithms run tests for you to review later." The disembodied voice responded.

"Such a life-saver." She tilted her head, scratching her scalp. "And nothing on the suspects in the HPF database. No matches on facial recognition, blood, or fingerprints. Either from out of town, or someone is really good at modifying records. Ayaka, see if we have any luck with the skimmer on matches with their faces on Current. Maybe we can ID them that way."

"Understood." The voice responded.

"Oh, and let's revisit the idea for some kind of pocket drone. Maybe even holo. If I could have had eyes in the sky, we could have made much better decisions. I don't want to be caught off guard again." The woman leaned back in her chair, supposedly taking in the data from the various displays.

"I hope I am not interrupting?" Amanda said. She smirked, pleased with the timing of her interjection.

The woman jumped in her seat, before whipping her head around to where Amanda was standing with Batou near the entrance. "Dear God. I'm sorry, I was miles away. Did you ask me something?"

Amanda came to sit across from the woman at the table, looking at her through several holo screens. She looked to be about Amanda's age. The shorter woman wore a blue blouse, and black, high waisted slacks with a black leather belt. Her dark, almond-shaped, slightly upturned, eyes looked Amanda over. "I trust you are Lieutenant Ichinose." Judging from how uncomfortable the hard metal chair was, this certainly was an interrogation room.

The woman visibly cringed as she cleared the screens away from between them. "Just call me Monica, if you don't mind."

"Not one for titles either, are you?"

"Can't say that I am, Ms. Amanda Marshall" Monica said, leaning back in her chair.

Amanda winced, which made the other woman smirk. "You know me?"

"Who doesn't know the princess of the city? Besides, I see the 'contributions' that get made whenever I submit a new report. You've made Chief Collins quite the wealthy man over the last couple years." She leaned forward and raised a hand to shield her mouth, as if telling a secret. "You know he's been looking at personal VTOLs so he can whizz around in style like the big wigs."

It was Amanda's turn to smirk. "Won't that be quite the sight?"

"My question is why? Why buy my reports?" Monica said, leaning back and crossing her legs. "Most trillionaires spend that kind of money on a yacht, some political candidate they want in office, or some kind of special steak from an endangered species."

"Interesting, and here I thought I was coming to ask *you* questions." Amanda said with chuckle.

The lieutenant sighed, and then shrugged. "Old habits, and such."

"Let's just say that I... have an interest in the Kitsune." Amanda said, crossing her arms over her chest.

"An interest deep enough to spend thousands of pounds to violate Records Law to get inconclusive, at best, case reports? I think there's better ways to waste your money, and break the law, to be frank." Monica said. "So, what are you then? Not a thrillseeker or you'd be out there trying to encounter her yourself. Not one of the thugs trying to take her out, or capture her as a bargaining chip, because you'd just work with one of the gangs or syndicates. Involving law enforcement would come with too many strings. So, why?" Something in the woman's tone told Amanda that she wasn't so much being interrogated, as she was genuinely curious. In another context, those same words might have come off as a threat, but not so from Monica.

"I just need to find her, that's all I'll say. I don't care what it takes, I just want her found, to be honest. Which brings me to why I am here." She leaned forward, her crossed arms resting on the cold metal table to support her weight. "You saw her, right?"

A smile crept up Monica's lips. "That I did. Just as far away from me as you are now." She leaned forward as well. "You know they were about to send me to the staff psychologist before you called the Chief. He thinks I've lost it, same thing with my Captain. His exact words were 'Obviously this firefight has you seeing things.'

A bucket of evidence is sitting there corroborating that the Kuroi Kitsune was there, and they are refusing to even consider it."

"Why wouldn't they believe you? You are in Special Crimes, this is literally what you do." Amanda asked.

Monica snorted. "As far as the brass is concerned, Special Crimes is a publicity stunt. A whole task force just for 'strange' and 'inexplicable' cases, most of which center around the Kitsune, and copycats. Do you know how many people are in the Special Crimes Task Force?"

"Can't say that I do," Amanda replied.

"One. Me. That's it. They even gave me the title of 'Head of Special Crimes' to make it sound more official. It's a joke to leadership." Monica said, laughing.

Amanda looked to Batou, and he nodded. He knew more about the internal office politics at the police force given that he worked with them directly to ensure her security, and to get 'priorities' taken care of.

"You going to introduce me to Chatty Kathy over there?" Monica asked.

Amanda smiled. "Of course, my apologies. This is my personal assistant, Ryuji Batou."

Batou bowed. Monica's eyes lingered on him for a moment before she said. "A pleasure." She considered a moment. "Former Pacific Alliance 15th Special Forces, aren't you?"

At this Batou grunted. "What gave me away?"

"Your tattoo on your right thumb" she said, gesturing with a tap to her own thumb, which did not have a tattoo. "Crossed axes behind a stylized cherry blossom. You must be a hell of a bodyguard."

Batou grunted again, but didn't add anything further.

"And you, am I undressed for this little chat, or something?" Monica gestured towards Amanda's clothing. She had worn a new black Avalonia open-backed dress adorned with clusters of crystal for the dedication and opening ceremony for the Space Elevator. It was a ridiculous thing to wear in her current setting.

Amanda smiled weakly. "I came straight from the opening of the Space Elevator."

"Oh, that's right, that was today, wasn't it?" Monica said, chuckling. "Easy to lose track of time in here."

"About that... why exactly are we in an interrogation room?" Amanda ask, looking around again at the austere chamber.

Monica smirked. "Oh, that. See, they didn't want to chance me giving them the slip in my office, or somehow getting myself plugged into the investigation into the attack. So, they've been grilling me all morning here."

"I must admit, I'm rather taken aback that they would set up your department just to say they have people working on these cases. Why waste anyone on something like this to begin with?" Amanda said, trying to steer the conversation back on course.

"I had to convince them to do it, to be honest. I told them it would be good PR to at least *look* like they were taking these cases seriously. Public opinion of the HPF was plummeting because people, rightly, I might add, thought that the police didn't care about the Kitsune, or these other strange cases, like with the Crimson Tengu, or the new one that's been popping up recently, the Golden Terror. So I argued that if they just made a department to investigate, they could get some pressure off of their backs." She chuckled, leaning back in her chair again. "It was an idea too good to pass up. They get to reap the PR, and throw the weirdo in a box."

"Weirdo?" Amanda asked, tilting her head to the side.

"Well, yeah. I'm the one who actually believes in this stuff," Monica said, "and I'm the one with wild ideas, like making robotic partners to act as force multipliers, or even replace boots on the ground entirely." He sighed, dismissing that idea with a wave of her hand. "Of course, the Proxy Accords make that hairy since autonomous systems are prohibited from violence unless a supervisor is present. But, on the more… legal side, how about making a companion AI to help officers analyze crime scenes. Or make holo flash forged body armor so officers would never be exposed without protection."

"Those sound like some pretty interesting ideas, if you ask me."

"See? But no, they just say it sounds too expensive, impractical, so on." Monica waved a hand in the air. Then made an impression in what Amanda guessed was meant to be Chief Collins voice and mannerisms "Oh, Ichinose. Something like that wouldn't be feasible on our budget. Please, Ichinose, that kind of thing just doesn't make sense."

Amanda thought for a moment, looking at the holo screens that were still up. Batou came behind her and pointed to a display that showed a diagram of body armor over the silhouette of a person. Formulae that Amanda immediately recognized, with arrows pointing to two red marks on the armor, described impact force that the armor had sustained. Then he pointed to another, one with programming code scrolling, and she realized that it was Gatesoft Mirror Deepscript. That was and artificial intelligence training script. Something clicked. "You made them anyway, didn't you? That Ayaka you were talking to is some kind of companion AI, isn't it?"

Monica jumped, then grinned mischievously. "Just as sharp as your mom, aren't you?"

"I try to be, at least. If they were so opposed to those ideas, how did you get them to fund development?"

At this Monica snorted, then chuckled. "I didn't. I've just been self-funding. Pretty much whatever I can scrounge together."

Amanda stared at Monica for a long while, considering. If there was one thing that she had inherited from the great Diana Marshall, it was the ability to sense a good opportunity. "Monica, what if *I* funded your ideas, maybe even got you some help for your investigations?"

Monica's dark eyes narrowed. She crossed her arms over her chest. "What's the catch?"

"No catch, not really. You get whatever financial backing you need to help with development, even help with patents and so on. I just want in on your tech, and your investigation reports on these Special Crimes cases." Amanda said.

"Chief Collins would never allow something like that." Monica said plainly. "Much less Bastion."

Amanda smirked. "Oh, I think you'll find him quite accommodating given the right... motivation. After all, those VTOL craft are so expensive to maintain. Also, I have a good relationship with Anton Bastion. He owes me a favor, one he is quite anxious for me to stop holding over his head."

Monica stood from her chair, looking at Amanda, then Batou, and then back to Amanda. She seemed to be looking for something. Perhaps a reason to not trust what was being offered.

"You won't interfere with my investigations?" she asked.

"I can't imagine why I would. I want answers, just like you." Amanda said, meeting Monica's eyes.

She stared back, and neither spoke for a long moment. Eventually Monica sat back down. "You are taking a pretty big risk on me. I could just be a quack with wacky ideas just like the Chief thinks."

"You could be, but I don't think you are." Amanda leaned back in her chair. "And if you ask me, Chief Collins's judgement only goes as far as who is filling his pocketbook. With the kind of ideas you've already told me, Bastion could have been making a killing. The holo body armor idea alone could revolutionize the defense industry, if it works out."

Monica burst into laughter, even smacking the table. "Oh, I knew I liked you."

She then stood, and held out her hand across the table. "You have a deal."

Amanda smiled as she stood, and shook Monica's hand. "We have a deal. We'll work out the details later." She then sat back down, and leaned forward. "Now, tell me everything"

DEFIANT HORIZON #3

Sleeping Tiger

The future is not given.
It is seized
By those whom
The present
Is found lacking.
Accept not what is.
Claim that which should be.

Byakko Industries Headquarters, Core Island, Hashishima City,
Hashishima,
Thursday, August 9th, 2035

Marko Byakko stood in the ruined lobby of his company's headquarters. Broken glass, chips of ultracrete, wood, blood, plastic bullet casings, and other debris littered the stark white marble floors. Bullet holes riddled the fine marble and slate walls. Seven security guards, and Gina, the night receptionist, had lost their lives in the attack, and three more guards were in the hospital. But why? Who would dare do something like this?

"Any update from HPF on how the hell they didn't see this as it was happening?" Marko said to his assistant in New Russian. He knelt to pick up a plastic casing, reading ArmaMaxx XFactor Tac7 printed in white on the dull grey surface.

"They are still investigating. Agent Greaves, with their CyberSec department is looking into the possibility of a cyber attack. Our techs have confirmed that the telecom line, and wireless was unaffected, and the Razorback that they used was not equipped with signal jammers. Seeing as other data from the building was unaffected, and no Loss of Signal alert was pinged in their system, a targeted cyber strike is most likely," Yura Sarkov, Marko's assistant said.

Marko frowned, and kicked at some debris on the floor. Glass skittered against the marble. He was furious, beyond furious. Anger burned in his chest, pushing him to act, to destroy, to make someone hurt. His accent grew thicker. "What about ID's on the mercs. Any orders found on them to indicate what they were after?"

"Nothing yet, sir. Even our own facial recognition AI couldn't identify them." Yura said, wincing at the sharp screech of the glass. "nothing in their pockets except for weapons, mostly from Defenstech, and hand tools."

He cursed, turned, and marched to the elevators. A final reminder of the attack, a bullet hole in the wall just around the corner from the elevators sparked Marko's anger again. "I don't trust them to figure this out. I want our people on this. If this was a strike from one of our competitors, we will pay them back a thousand-fold."

"I've already got Romanov and Braun on it." Yura said as they stepped onto the waiting elevator.

Marko nodded. "I want Chang on it too."

"Understood, sir. Sending orders now." Yura said, typing away at her holo console.

They stood in silence as they ascended. Marko cracked his gnarly knuckles, trying to cool his anger. He wanted to raze the city to find who had the audacity to attack his company. He would do it, too, if he felt it would get him any closer to an answer. More likely he would burn anyone who knew anything in the process, and have even less to go on than he did before.

As the door opened to his office, he said. "I want patrol drones on constant surveillance around the perimeter. Set up our company of AutoMatik infantry bots we've been working on for the Future Combat Initiative ready to be deployable at a moment's notice on every point of entry. Authorize armor piercing ammo, shotguns, and KA-449's for the security team. This will not happen again."

"Sir," Yura started, sighing, "I don't think the police will like us deploying military hardware like that."

"They let us get attacked, an attack that cost eight of my people their lives. They can deal with it, or I'll buy up Bastion's contract and do their job myself if they don't like it." Marko said. He sat at his massive stainless-steel desk, and took out a cigar from his pinstripe suit jacket, a Rubio Especial. "They are lucky I'm not bringing tanks. And if they don't want to do their job, I'll call Petersburg, and had the streets flooded with OSP agents."

Yura sat at the corner of his desk, which always made her look like a porcelain doll with her petite proportions, and pale white skin, in contrast to size of the gargantuan desk. Most would have called his desk a conference table. To Marko it was almost big enough to serve as his desk. When he really needed to think, he printed out all of the data he needed to consider, and splayed them out across his desk.

She put a hand on his shoulder. "Marko, we are going to figure out who did this, and we will deal with them."

He cut the cigar tip, lit it, sat back in his cool steel chair, and puffed on the cigar. The acrid smoke teased his throat, helping him feel more himself again. "We better. We need to send a message." Marko said, smoke billowing out of his mouth as he spoke.

Yura snatched his cigar and took a long drag for herself before handing it back.

Marko sighed, meeting her icy blue eyes. "We don't have time for that right now."

"Too bad," Yura said with a smirk.

Marko looked her over again, golden hair pulled into a tight bun, tight black pant suit hugging her slight figure in all the right ways. Thin lips, and sharp nose. Just like...

He stood, scratched at his shaved head, and puffed the cigar again. "Push back the meeting for Transference. Push everything back. Call Viktor in." Then he turned away from her, and walked to his old record player that sat on a metal bookshelf behind his chair. He set "Anthems of Victory" by Yeltsin on the player, and turned up the volume. Then he started to pace as a brisk, inspiring march barked in his cavernous office. It was called "Forward, for the Motherland."

After a while, his cigar nearly gone, he heard the familiar nasal voice of Viktor, speaking in New Russian. "You still listen to this shit?"

Marko looked over to a mountain of a man, mounds of muscles barely contained in a red alligator leather jacket. He cursed. "You never have had any sense of taste."

"You don't pay me to have taste for all this old shit." Viktor said, crossing his arms.

"No, I pay you to keep the other organizations from moving against us, keeping shit like what happened last night from happening. This 'old shit' is your cultural heritage, have some respect." Marko said.

Viktor laughed and shook his head. "I say let it burn. We burned plenty in the Ascension"

"Well, we should be so lucky you don't get to decide that." Marko replied, then nodded to a seat at his desk. Viktor sat as suggested, leaning back in the chair.

Marko sat back down, and offered a cigar, to which Viktor waved a refusal, before extracting a cigarette from his jacket, and lighting it. Marko sighed. "And I expect you still drink that cheap goat piss vodka you always do?"

Viktor laughed, took a long drag on his cigarette, and then said, "And why not? It's available, you can buy a lot, and if you drink enough, you forget about your problems just the same."

"One day I'll get through to you on just how much better the good stuff is."

"And you forget what it's like to not even be able to afford the cheap shit," Viktor said, taking another drag. "What I drink and smoke now was the stuff of kings to us back then. Hell, even a scrap of bread was a small fortune to us."

Marko shook his head. "Believe me, I haven't forgotten, nor will I." He puffed on the cigar one last time, and then snuffed out what little was left on an ashtray.

"Why did you call me here? The merc company attack?" Viktor asked.

Marko nodded. "The police are doing whatever it is they do, I have some my best looking into it, but your people can get where they can't, can talk to people mine can't."

"And how will you make it worth the Kusnetsov's time?" Viktor said with a nonchalant tone.

"For one, it *is* what I pay you for. But, do this, find out who attacked me, and I'll get you those weapons you have been asking for," Marko said. "assault rifles, drones, explosives—"

"What about those fighting robots you've been working on?" Viktor interrupted.

Marko's eyes narrowed. "How do you know about that?"

Viktor chuckled, and took a long drag on his cigarette. "We all have our ways of knowing things we shouldn't," He leaned forward on the desk, "I won't ask about yours if you don't ask about mine."

Marko considered for a long while, tapping his fingers on the desk as he thought, then said, "Find them, bring them to me, alive, and we'll talk. It is a program still in development, so there are things to consider."

"One regiment, when they are ready." Viktor put out his cigarette on the steel desk, purposefully *next to* the ashtray, and stood from his chair.

"When they are ready." Marko held out his hand, and Viktor shook it.

"We'll start hitting the streets. The Kusnetsovs always get results." Viktor turned to leave.

Marko nodded. "I'm counting on it." The elevator door closed behind Viktor, and he was gone.

Yura stepped back in from the wet bar around the corner with a pair of glasses. She handed one to him, and he gulped down the vodka. He groaned as the cool liquid burned down his throat.

"Marko, are you sure about this?" Yura said, then knocked back her own glass.

"I don't care how the dogs who did this are found, I just want to watch the life drain from their eyes myself. If I have to unleash the wolves to do it, so be it." Marko said. He could feel his anger building again, mixed with the burn of the vodka in his stomach. "What else do I pay them for? He has as much to make up to me as the Police. They both failed to prevent this."

"No," Yura started, "I mean promising him AutoMatik. What would the Kusnetsovs want with a regiment of robotic soldiers?"

"Probably finally take over this town, pushing out the other gangs. It doesn't matter, it's beneath us." Mark felt his anger near bursting out of his chest. He started breathing heavily, and his body suddenly felt so cold. The music on the record player warped and distorted as he fell over, barely catching himself from falling on the desk. Yura said something, but he couldn't make it out. Nothing made any sense. Up, down, colors, why was he trying to stand up anyway?

Then his grip on the desk slipped. He was falling...

VENTURE BEYOND

STORIES FROM HIDDEN WORLDS

Short Story Podcast

SCI-FI Fantasy HORROR

      12

Made in the USA
Monee, IL
20 November 2025

34094327R00056